WHEN THE FRONT DOOR CLOSES

Doreen Hedges

MINERVA PRESS

LONDON
ATLANTA   MONTREUX   SYDNEY

WHEN THE FRONT DOOR CLOSES
Copyright © Doreen Hedges 1998

ISBN 1 86106 946 4

First Published 1998 by
MINERVA PRESS
195 Knightsbridge
London SW7 1RE

Printed in Great Britain for Minerva Press

WHEN THE FRONT DOOR CLOSES

Acknowledgements

My thanks to:

Chief Inspector Lund (retired) and Police Constable Whybrew (retired) for their help and advice.

Also to Sally Jane Danter for her guidance on psychic matters.

My thanks also to my sister, Daphne, for her efforts in writing the original script when I was unable to do so.

Lastly to Elizabeth Milne for typing the story from the many pages of my indecipherable handwriting.

Part One

Chapter One

1971

When I first saw the house I felt a chill down my spine. It wasn't unpleasant, the paintwork was newly done and the roof well-kept. I could tell that work had been done in the garden too. No, the house looked well cared for all right, but still I could feel a chill down my spine and an awful foreboding. Anyone who can read the atmosphere of a place will know what I mean. It is not something you can explain easily, especially to people who cannot or will not understand. So I didn't say anything to Jack, my husband, knowing he would laugh if I did. The family had always been amused at my 'feelings' as they call them, but no one laughs now.

The house agent walked along the path and I thought, He looks uneasy, I wonder why. Is it the house? Anyway, he bustled around showing us over the place and keeping up the patter of words which are his trade. He certainly worked hard to get a sale.

Jack was pleased with everything he saw and even more pleased to think he was getting a house at a much lower figure than its obvious worth.

'Why is the price so low?' I asked.

'The vendor had to return north because of family sickness,' the agent replied smoothly.

That's a well-rehearsed line, I thought.

'Well, Laura, this place is a bargain,' Jack said to me. 'I think we'll buy it.'

I was panic-stricken. What could I do to stop him buying the house? If I told Jack I knew there was something wrong he would want to know exactly what was wrong, and what could I say to that? I just knew.

'Jack, I don't like it here, please let's go somewhere else,' I said.

'Look, Laura, we've been searching for weeks now and we'll never get another chance as good as this one.' Jack turned to the agent. 'I'll ring you this afternoon, Mr Greaves, and tell you one way or another.'

I knew then what his answer would be: we would buy the house. I could almost feel the malevolent smile of the place and could almost hear it say, 'I've been waiting for you, but you won't stay long, no one ever does, I see to that.'

Who is it? I thought. Who does not wish us to live here?

Anyway, we moved in and had been living there for about six or eight weeks. Jack had teased me about my misgivings and I had to admit to a certain pride in the decor. As we hadn't had to spend as much on buying the house, we were able to give more to the furnishings. I still wasn't at ease but had begun to think my feelings had been wrong this time.

I had spoken to a few women who were neighbours and they were all friendly until I asked them in for coffee or tea; then they always had to dash somewhere or had a previous engagement and couldn't get away from me quickly enough, I could tell by the look on their faces. This of course added to my certainty that there was a mystery surrounding the house.

I had made it clear to Jack that I wouldn't spend any time alone at night in the house. I wasn't happy on my own in the daytime, let alone the night. I was adamant about this; if he had to go away overnight I would go to a hotel or stay with relatives if I couldn't go with him.

Our life settled down to a routine existence. The summer had almost finished and I was thinking it would soon be time to clear the gardens ready for planting again. Jack had come in from work at six and we were just finishing dinner when there was a terrific crash from the kitchen. We both dashed out there, only to find nothing amiss, but I did fancy I heard someone laughing. We went back to the dining room to finish our coffee.

'Did you hear someone laugh?' I asked Jack.

He looked uncomfortable and replied, 'No,' but I knew he was lying.

We cleared up after our meal and sat down to watch television. Just as the news was starting we heard furniture being moved upstairs.

'Must be next door,' Jack said, but when we went upstairs we found our bedroom in complete disarray. I knew then that I had been right all along and that there was something very wrong in the house. During that night and the next day everything was peaceful. I had been on edge all day, feeling that I was being watched and that the watcher was not friendly.

I shall remember the next night as long as I live. All was quiet until we got into bed. We settled down to sleep and suddenly the bedclothes were pulled away from us. We sat up and I put on the over-bed light and as I did so the bedroom door flew open and slammed shut. Then we heard that dreadful laughter again. Without warning things on the dressing table were swept to the floor and the bedroom chair toppled over.

Jack and I literally fell out of bed in our haste to get to the door. As we ran down the stairs and out of the front door, the small table on the landing was thrown down the stairs. We could still hear that maniacal laughter.

We were at the gate now, clinging to one another. We turned to look back at the house and the front door slammed shut. We could still hear furniture being moved around and crockery breaking. It was like being awake but in a nightmare at the same time.

The lights were on in the house next door. Their front door opened and someone came out. I could see them out of the corner of my eye as they came down the path but just could not tear my eyes away from our house. I realised Jack was still holding my arm and we were both trembling.

'Mrs Gordon,' said a voice. 'Mrs Gordon, come in with us.' That broke the spell and I turned to see my neighbour, Fay.

The next thing I remember was waking up in a strange room and someone was saying, 'Drink this, dear, it will do you good.' I drank whatever it was and choked at the taste, I never did care for brandy. When I looked around for Jack I saw that he looked very grey and shaken. He was also very annoyed.

'Mrs Oliver has just told me that this has happened before, quite often before. I'm going to see that estate agent and find out why he didn't tell me the truth. The last owners didn't have go north at all, they had to leave the house for the same reason we did.'

I looked at Fay. 'Is that why you would never come into the house?' I asked.

She looked quickly at her husband and then back at me. 'You had peaceful days. The three couples before you were troubled in the daytime as well.'

'Thank God we didn't have the boys with us. I don't think I would even have thought of them at that awful moment, would you, Jack?' I asked my husband.

'Probably not,' he said, 'but probably yes.'

Our sons, Robert and Peter, were away at boarding school and for that I was heartily thankful. Jack may have thought about them in the stress of that moment but I wasn't at all sure I would have, and yet if there had been a fire I am sure I would have tried to get the children out safely. This sort of thing was beyond anything that one usually connects with danger.

'Drink up your brandy, dear,' said Jack, breaking into my thoughts.

John Oliver came to take my glass.

'Strangely,' he said, 'whatever it is that is disturbing that house has never troubled the children. Mr and Mrs Peters had two children and they were never frightened. Do you remember, Fay, little Jane used to talk about the tall man she had seen? The Peters used to think it was her imagination until they were disturbed.'

'Aren't you ever frightened living next door; how long have you lived here anyway?' I know my question sounded a bit rude but it just seemed to pop out.

'We've been here about six years, haven't we, Fay? Nothing has disturbed us, except the noise of course. The Reverend Marshall was called in to do an exorcism twice but that only made things worse. Whatever or whoever is causing all the trouble seemed to be infuriated by it all.'

I didn't realise Fay had left the room and when, a few moments later, the door opened, I jumped. She had made more tea for us all and told Jack and I that she had made up beds in the spare room and thought we should get some sleep or we'd be fit for nothing in the morning. I realised then that we were only in our night-clothes and hadn't stopped to put on dressing gowns.

Chapter Two

Fortunately the next day was Saturday and Jack didn't have to go to work. I awoke feeling exhausted, and looking at Jack I knew he felt the same. We knew we would have to go back into the house if only to get dressed.

'Jack,' I said, 'I'm not living in there again until something is done to clear the place of its ghost.'

Jack put his arms around me. 'No, love, I wouldn't ask you to, and I certainly don't want another night like last night either. We'd both go off our heads if we stayed there as it is.'

We put on the dressing gowns we had borrowed and went downstairs. What we would have done without our good neighbours I do not know. Not only did they let us stay that night, but they suggested we stayed at least over the weekend.

Both Jack and I were filled with dread as we approached the house that morning. We had got to the door before we realised we couldn't get in. In our haste to leave last night we hadn't even thought about keys, or money, nor anything else except to get out as quickly as we could. We had no idea what would greet us when we went in, and although we had heard enough noise when we stood at the gate, we were, nevertheless, unprepared for the devastation.

We had to break a window in the door to get to the lock. Jack looked through the hole. 'My God,' he breathed. 'I wish I could spare you this,' he said to me, 'but you'll have to collect what you want too.'

As he put his hand in to open the door I could feel my heart racing. I couldn't believe my eyes. The whole place was a shambles. We went from room to room, first downstairs and then through the bedrooms.

Furniture was overturned in every room, all our ornaments were on the floor, some were broken into small pieces. The kitchen would take an age to clear up. Wherever we went it was the same. From fear my feelings changed to pure anger. I stood in our bedroom surrounded by chaos. Blinding rage smothered me. I could hardly breathe.

'If you think you will get rid of me you can think again!' I was screaming. I clenched my fists and raised them above my head. 'I'll fight you every way I can. I'll never give up if I die in the attempt. God help me.' I could feel tears on my cheeks, but they were tears of rage, not sorrow, at that moment. 'I'm going to get you out of our house, *our house*. The house is ours, not yours, and it's time you realised it.'

I packed a suitcase for each of us, collected my handbag and jewellery, and Jack and I went back to the Olivers' house. I was seething and could hardly wait to return to our house to get it cleared up.

As it happened, we spent more than that weekend sleeping next door. I cleaned up the house and cleared the debris that day and was not disturbed at all. What I didn't know then was that there would be a lot more damage done and a deal more clearing up to do as well. Many nights I cried myself to sleep but remained just as determined not to give in.

The local newspaper somehow got hold of the story and then the nationals sent reporters. They wanted to hold seances in the house, but I felt this was only a publicity stunt, and anyway I knew it was the wrong thing to do.

Without being told, I knew that whoever it was causing all the trouble and heartache needed help. If our guest had been alive, he or she would have been sent away to get medical care. I felt that our guest or ghost needed help just as much.

The solution to our problem came as a result of the publicity given to the hauntings by the national newspapers. Jack and I received many letters from people who said they were ghost hunters and wanted to visit the house. There always seemed to be a number of people standing outside looking and some even trampled over the gardens to look in the windows.

About two weeks after the first disturbances, there was a suggestion in a newspaper report that perhaps we were trying a publicity stunt, and another which stated that we had played around with a Ouija board. We ignored all the snide remarks but were upset by them. Even our kind friends Mr and Mrs Oliver came in for criticism.

Strangely, although it had been reported that we were spending the nights sleeping next door, there were no attempted burglaries. I suppose a thief didn't want to risk being dealt with by a ghost, so at least we had that to be thankful for.

Robert and Peter, our sons, were by now clamouring to be allowed home, at least for a weekend. Fortunately Jack agreed with me and refused their requests.

Chapter Three

We would soon have to make up our minds over what we were going to do, either sell the house, if this were possible, or live in it again properly. We were not keen on either prospect.

Mr and Mrs Oliver were still agreeable to us sleeping in their house, although I knew this must be a strain on them. But with the colder weather coming soon we would have to make up our minds or we would be coping with frozen and burst pipes.

Then, one morning, a letter came, addressed to us and sent care of Mr and Mrs Oliver. It was sent from a Mrs Bant, who said she was a medium who had in the past been useful in clearing haunted places of the disturbing entity. She said she belonged to a 'rescue service' meaning that the 'rescue' was the rescue of the haunting entity from its earthbound state. This could also be applied to the person or persons who were being haunted.

It all sounded most peculiar to me and I showed the letter to Jack.

'It does sound a bit odd,' he said, 'but I think we ought to consider it. It can't do any harm to discuss it with Mr and Mrs Oliver.'

They were as much in the dark as we were, but thought it was worth looking into.

'We can't stay here indefinitely,' said Jack. 'I think you've been more than good friends as it is.'

'Perhaps we can invite her over to discuss it,' I said. 'If the distance from where she lives is too far, we could pay for her to stay in the hotel for as long as is necessary.'

It was decided that I should write to invite her over the following weekend and this I did.

I expected Mrs Bant to be an odd-looking woman. I had never met a medium before and had always thought they were a bit queer in the head. She had written to say she only went on the rescue service accompanied by her husband, and would be grateful if I would arrange for a minister of religion to be present.

I duly went along to see the Reverend Marshall, who seemed a bit put out that we had not come to him before, but he agreed to join us. We sat in the Olivers' sitting room. Mr and Mrs Oliver, Jack and me, and the Reverend Marshall, and waited for the arrival of Mr and Mrs Bant. When their car drew up in front of the gate and a young good-looking man got out followed by a beautiful blonde woman, I think we were all stunned.

'She's not a bit like I pictured her to be,' I said.

'You can say that again,' said Mr Oliver.

I went to open the door for them. They came breezily into the sitting room and I introduced them to everyone.

'You'd like some tea?' said Fay. I had now come to use Mrs Oliver's first name as I spent so much time with her. I went out to the kitchen to help her with the tea things. When we returned, Mr and Mrs Bant were chatting freely to the Reverend Marshall about their work. He seemed to be as much in the dark about it as we were and did not seem to be very happy about being involved.

Mrs Bant said, 'We can have a sitting in your house, Mrs Gordon. I shall go into a trance and my guides will contact the entity who has disturbed you.'

Her husband told us that it might be very unpleasant and probably frightening and that we would need perhaps more than one sitting. Whatever happened during the sitting, he implied that we must not panic, and he told us that they had a number of guides working with them and they were strong.

'They will give us all the help they can,' he said.

Mr Bant looked at the vicar. 'We would like you, sir, to start the sitting with a short service but not an exorcism. Are you agreeable to that?'

'I think we would like to know a bit more about it all first,' I said.

'Yes, that's true,' said Reverend Marshall. 'I have already tried an exorcism service twice, but to no avail. It seems to me there is something really evil in that house. I don't wish to get involved in any hocus-pocus or black magic rituals.'

'Not evil, and truly there are no black magic rituals,' said Mrs Bant. 'Whoever is in there is mentally disturbed, just as we have people living on this Earth who are mentally disturbed and do violent things. Whoever it is, they are probably more to be pitied than blamed.'

'It is difficult for people to understand what happens after death,' said Mrs Bant. 'Sometimes a person who has died becomes what we call earthbound either because they are unable to realise they are dead, simply because they do not expect to be exactly as they were, you see, or because they could become earthbound because there are ties here which they cannot or will not give up. I am not going to give you a talk on life after death though. I have only mentioned the two possibilities to give possible reasons for what has occurred. We are willing to try to help if you wish, but we want to make it clear we cannot promise success.'

'When would you like to do it?' asked Jack. Mr Bant indicated that they could start today.

We were all taken aback by this. I didn't like being rushed and suggested tomorrow if that was all right with everyone else. Finally we agreed that the sitting or seance would take place the next afternoon, which was Saturday.

When Jack and I went into the house the next morning it looked as if a typhoon had struck it. As I had already cleared up the place four times over the past week I was thoroughly fed up with the whole thing.

'I can't face much more,' I wept. 'I feel like going over the house myself and breaking things up.'

Jack looked at me and grinned. 'If you can't beat 'em, join 'em,' he said. I had to admit it had a sort of logic!

Mr and Mrs Bant said they would come at about 5 p.m., and Fay and her husband agreed to join us. Reverend Marshall could not come before this time because he had marriage services to conduct. I wished we could have avoided the whole thing, but knew I could never live in that house again as things were.

We all met in the Olivers' home and decided we would go into our house through the back door, in the hope that we would not be noticed. None of us wanted a stream of reporters around. Creeping furtively through the back garden, we went into our kitchen.

All was peaceful and serene then. There was nothing out of place as far as I could see, either in the kitchen or in the sitting room. As every house-proud person will know, we like other people to see our homes neat and tidy, and I was no exception, even under the present circumstances. Still, I felt we were being watched.

'You have a lovely home, Mr Gordon,' said Mrs Bant. 'It is so light and airy.'

'It cost me quite bit to decorate it,' said Jack. 'Of course, it is not as nice now as when we first had it done, but you know why that is.' It was true. The paintwork showed what could only be called 'battle scars'.

'After Jack returned from the army we looked around for a place we could settle in for the rest of our lives,' I said. 'We can reach the country or the town easily from here. It would be so nice to feel happy here.'

Mr Bant looked round our sitting room, and then at me. 'Could we have chairs arranged in a circle, please? Do you mind if we start?'

When we had arranged our chairs to the satisfaction of Mr and Mrs Bant, we were told to put on all the lights in case dusk set in before we had finished the sitting.

Chapter Four

When we were all seated, the Reverend Marshall, remaining seated at Mr Bant's request, asked us to join him in a prayer. We all said the Lord's Prayer and he asked for a blessing on us all.

Mr Bant then continued by asking our Spiritual Father for His love and protection for us all. I cannot remember all the words he used, or exactly what happened, but I will do my best to give as clear on account as I can.

Mr Bant continued by saying, 'Father, spirit of love, we ask for help and guidance for those in the spirit world who come to aid us in our rescue work, and we ask for help for the one who remains in this house disturbing the peace and tranquillity which is so desired by Laura and Jack Gordon.'

Speaking to us all sitting in the circle, he said, 'Will you join with me please in your thoughts? Will you all ask sincerely for help for the earthbound entity who remains in this house? Keep this thought constantly in your mind, and by doing so you will help our guides and spirit helpers to do their work.'

I noticed then that Mrs Bant appeared to be asleep. She was breathing quite deeply, but in a short while this changed to very shallow breathing. I did not see her lips move but then I heard a male voice say, 'God bless you.'

Mr Bant replied, 'God bless you.'

The first speaker, who had a slight Continental accent, I thought, then said, 'We have joined you today to try to help you. It will not be easy but we will do our best. You must do as you are told by the husband of the lady whom I speak through. Continue your good thoughts, for they will help us.'

There was a crash in the room above and we all jumped.

'Do not be alarmed,' said the voice and then seemed to speak to the area by the door. 'Tell us why you object to these people living here, friend.'

Mrs Bant became restless and rose from her chair and started pacing up and down.

'I'm not your *friend*, mate, never seen you before, and as for them they don't belong here. No one who comes here belongs here. I don't want anyone else here, the place is mine.' The voice was strong and the words disjointed.

'I got this place for my Glenda but she wasn't satisfied with it. Yes, and then one day she walked out, taking the kids with her. I'd worked hard for her and nothing I ever did was good enough. So she found someone else.' The pacing stopped. 'That didn't last long though, I saw to that.' The terrible laughter started again and with it the words were repeated over and over again. 'Yes, I saw to that, didn't last long, didn't last long.'

The Continental voice spoke then. 'Friend, the good people who have come to live in this house want to make it their home. They too have children and want them to live here. Can you not forgive what has happened in the past and help them?'

Mrs Bant then sat down, but not for long. There was silence for a while, then, 'I don't give a toss about their kids or any other kids. They're nothing but a bloody nuisance anyway.'

Mr Bant then spoke. 'When you came here to live with your family, you wanted the house to be a home, didn't you? Now you have left your Earth life – you have, you know – it would be much better for you to go on to our Father God's kingdom. God loves you and these lovely souls who have been with you through the week want to take you there.'

I think it was at this point that Mrs Bant started pacing around again. 'You're talking rubbish. I've not left this life, I'm still here and I'm still me. I still make people take notice of me, don't I? If I were dead I couldn't do that, could I?' The voice rose to screaming pitch. 'I tried to commit suicide after I'd done away with Glenda's man friend. Yes, I dealt with him.' Then he started to laugh again, that terrible senseless laugh.

I looked at the others sitting in the room with me. Fay and her husband were holding hands tightly. The Reverend Marshall was gripping the seat of his chair as if he were afraid he would fall, and Jack had his hands clasped together as if he were straining to keep calm. I don't really know how I felt except that it had a dream-like quality about it, perhaps I should say nightmare instead.

'Would you like me to tell you how I dealt with the boyfriend, eh, would you?' Mrs Bant sat down. 'I knifed him until I couldn't find anywhere else to put the knife. He thought I was coming for a nice friendly talk.' There was silence and I felt he was thinking about what he had done, for he (or rather Mrs Bant) was smiling slightly. I shuddered and felt sick.

Then Mrs Bant started pacing again. 'Then I thought I'd finish myself off too, but I couldn't do that until I'd done away with his body.' He seemed to be more excited at this point. 'I'm not talking to you anymore, bloody nosy parkers. What are you all doing here anyway? Who asked you to come?'

Mrs Bant seemed to slide to the floor. I made a move to help her, but Mr Bant told me to stay where I was. Then the Continental voice spoke once more.

'Do not be afraid, friends. We will take care of our little lady here. We have much work to do to help you, the poor man is very disturbed. We will try to persuade him to leave with us, but he needs much convincing that he has died from Earth life. We will need to meet again soon. God bless you all.'

Then there was silence. Mr Bant put his hand up to indicate we must be quiet. Mrs Bant was still on the floor but was waking from her sleep state.

Mr Bant said, 'We thank you, Heavenly Father, for your love and protection, and we thank also our spirit friends for joining us. May the peace which comes from our Father in Heaven remain with us at all times.'

Mrs Bant was making sighing noises, and she tried to sit up. Her husband went to help her, saying, 'When you are ready, dear, we will go back next door.'

Some thirty minutes later we were in Fay's sitting room having tea. Mrs Bant asked what had happened and we were all doing our best to tell her. Then the noise started up in our house. There were crashes and bangs as if a terrible fight was taking place. Fortunately the house is the end one in the road and stands back a good way, so the noise would not be heard by neighbours.

I asked Fay, 'Is this what you have had to put up with all this time?'

She said, 'Yes, but it hasn't happened very often. After all, no one remained for long. When it was empty, there was peace.'

Mr Bant said, 'If you'll take my advice, you will not go back in there again until we have completed our task, it would not be safe.'

We arranged a date and time for another sitting, which was to be in two weeks, again on a Saturday. Jack and I continued to live with Fay and John Oliver. It was a relief to me not to have to return to that house. I did not want to go in there even in daylight, and the thought of sleeping in there filled me with horror.

I did not want to return for the next sitting with Mr and Mrs Bant, but above my fear was still the determination to have the house to ourselves and I did not care how long it took. Little did I know then how much heartache was to come.

I kept thinking of what the disturbed person – the ghost, I suppose – had said about stabbing his wife's boyfriend to death. Where had he done this and where was the body? The thought kept going round and round in my brain.

Also, his suicide of course. Where had he done this? Somehow I must find out the answers. If I went to the local newspaper offices we would be pestered with reporters again, and I didn't want that. If I went to the police there would be endless questions, and I didn't think we could face that yet. What of the man's wife? I wondered what she had done when the boyfriend didn't return to her.

As the days went by and Saturday grew closer, I became more and more tense. I needed to work and Fay seemed to understand this. She let me work on whatever I fancied, cleaning, washing, gardening, anything to keep me occupied. She was truly understanding and I shall always be grateful. The urge to find out the whole story remained with me. I decided to wait until after the next sitting on

Saturday and if that didn't answer some of the questions in my mind I would have to do some investigating myself.

Jack was not very happy being a lodger in someone else's house, but as neither of us was very keen to return to our own home just yet, he had to accept the situation with good grace. We did not hear any further noise from next door, but we did not go to see what damage had been done either. I thought we might as well let 'him', whoever he was, get on with what he seemed to enjoy doing for the time being, but I was determined that this situation would not go on indefinitely. I wondered if we ought to have the furniture removed, but decided that at the moment this would almost admit defeat, and that I would not allow.

Chapter Five

Jack awoke first on Saturday morning. I had had a rather sleepless night and was late in waking up. I realised it was Saturday, and a feeling of near panic swept over me.

Jack said, 'Well, this is the day, dear.' He sounded tired and tense at the same time. 'Look, Laura, if you wish I can sell the house. We can go right away from here. You need never go in there again.' Jack took my hand. 'Tell me what you want me to do,' he said.

I thought, And give in to that man in there? Straight away I realised that 'the man in there' wasn't alive as we are alive here.

'Jack,' I said, 'I would love to give in and sell the house, but really that wouldn't help us or anyone who came after us, would it?'

Jack moved away from the bed. He said, 'I'm not thinking of anyone else. Whoever came after us would have to cope with it themselves. I'm thinking of us. We can't go on living like this. Fay and John are wonderful to have to put up with us as it is. It's not fair to them at all. They have a right to live on their own in their own home.' He turned to face me. 'How long are we going to go on like this?'

I got out of bed and went over to him. 'Jack, dear, listen to me. Let's see what happens this afternoon. We must give Mr and Mrs Bant a chance to do what they say they can do.'

Jack put his arms around me. 'Laura, can't you see? If I had listened to you in the first place, we wouldn't be in this mess.'

'Jack, don't say that.' The tears welled up in my eyes. 'You know that where you go, I go. It's always been that way and always will be. Come, let's get dressed and go downstairs.'

We were all dressed and waiting for Mr and Mrs Bant by four o'clock. None of us had eaten very much as I think we all felt too nervous.

Reverend Marshall arrived looking pale and anxious. I realised then that he wasn't a young man and didn't really understand what was happening, Then I knew with a shock that I understood perfectly what it was all about. My 'feelings' were a means of being told things that others couldn't know or see.

We had seated ourselves in the same position as before. I was relieved that our sitting room wasn't in too bad a state, considering the noise after our last sitting.

At least the furniture was still intact. It was dusk, but we had put on the lights and drawn the curtains back and front so that we could not be seen.

Mr Bant said the same words as before and soon Mrs Bant was 'asleep'. After a short while the Continental voice spoke. 'God bless you,' it said, to which Mr Bant replied, 'God bless you.'

'Good friends,' said our Continental speaker, 'thank you for coming once more. We have been with our disturbed friend through the time since we last met you. He is a very unhappy man. He will not accept his passing from the physical life. He is not an evil man, but a sick man, sick to his soul, I fear. Even after we have taken him away from here, he will need much love and care. All that he dearly loved has been taken from him. His love was a selfish love, no doubt, but he has suffered because of it. Pity him and send out good thoughts to him, whatever he says or does.'

We heard the now familiar violent noises from upstairs.

'My helpers are trying to bring him down to us now.'

'Leave me alone' was shouted from outside the room. 'What are you doing in my house? Who invited you all?' The door was flung open.

'Come, friend,' said the Continental voice, 'talk to us. Let these people talk with you. They want to help you.'

'I don't need any of you. Why don't you all go away.' Mrs Bant got up and paced the room.

I spoke then. 'Why won't you go with these people who have been here through the week? They want to help you and only have your welfare at heart.'

Mrs Bant swung round to face me. 'And why don't you mind your own bloody business and leave me alone! I'm not going anywhere away from this house. You want me out of the way so you can stay here instead. Well, sod you! I'll deal with you as I have dealt with all the others.'

'Friend.' The Continental voice spoke again. 'This good lady came to live here with her husband and wants to bring her children here. You have left the physical life and now you belong with us in the spirit world.'

'Don't make me laugh.' Mrs Bant sat down. 'You're trying again to tell me I'm dead, I suppose. How can I be dead when I can see myself and feel myself as well as I can see everyone else? The boyfriend's dead though, I made sure of that.' He gave that terrible laugh again. 'He's in the forest. There won't be much left of his body now. It was quite a while ago.' Mrs Bant sat down and seemed to be wearing a half-smile.

I said, 'Well, this is 1971. When did you deal with him?'

'Don't be funny,' he said, 'who are you trying to kid? I killed him in September 1964. I told you what I did, didn't I? Yes, I did, I know I did. I'm not talking to you idiots anymore.' Mrs Bant got out of her chair. 'I'm going upstairs and I want you out of here. Go on, sod off, and leave me alone.' Mrs Bant slid to the floor and the door slammed shut.

The Continental voice spoke once more. 'I must go to him. Thank you all and God bless you.'

Mrs Bant started moaning softly. She gradually woke up and her husband went to her.

We heard terrible crashes from above us. I said to Jack, 'We are not going to have much of our house left at this rate.'

One week later we were preparing for another sitting. We had not been into our house throughout the week. There had been plenty of noise from there and I knew if we ventured in, things would only get worse. There could not be very much left that was not broken. So far, the noise had come from upstairs, but I hoped we still had some furniture left downstairs, however I knew it would not be long before that suffered the same fate.

During the time between sittings I did some research. Every day when I could I went either to the library to look at the local papers, or to the newspaper library in London to go through the national newspapers, where I read everything I could from 1964. Anything which appeared relevant I wrote down in a notebook.

I'd learned that there were three men reported missing during 1964 from around the district, but I did not know which one might be the 'boyfriend' about whom we had heard next door.

I thought at one time we should ask the local police to send someone to join us in the sittings, but then rejected the idea, thinking they would not take it seriously. To me it was serious, not only for Jack and me, but for the poor soul who was tied to the house next door. Anyway I decided to ask at the next sitting about this.

As the time grew nearer I felt more and more tense. It was like being in a perpetual nightmare from which there was no awakening.

Fay and John were as helpful as ever, but I knew they felt the strain also. I worried in case 'he' came into this house, and thought I must get their feelings on this.

We were bothered occasionally by odd people telephoning and making stupid or insulting remarks, but at least we were not bothered by pressmen now.

As always, time does not stand still, even when we wish it would, and so the time came for us to go into our house.

We seated ourselves in our usual circle, and as before started with prayers. I did not know that at the previous sittings the Bants had brought a small tape recorder with them, and I noticed it for the first time tonight.

The person with the Continental voice spoke to us very soon after the prayers. He said he was so sorry to leave us so suddenly last week, but hoped we understood the reason for this. He also said that this sitting might well be difficult and upsetting. We had no doubt gathered that our disturbed friend had been very noisy in the last few days. They had tried to calm him but had had very little success.

We then heard the terrible laughter again coming from upstairs and there were very noisy crashes and bangs. 'He' sounded quite maniacal and I wondered if we would come away from this sitting unscathed. I worried quite correctly: we didn't!

We heard him yelling loud enough for all the street to hear, it seemed.

'You damned interfering busybodies. I'll teach you all a lesson, I won't have you coming in here as if you owned the place.' We heard more crashes and bangs and then the door burst open. Without warning, furniture toppled over and the few ornaments that were left were thrown about the room, during which the voice screamed out, 'Get out, get out, bloody interfering busybodies. I'll kill you, that's what I'll do, bastards, the lot of you.'

We all sat glued to our chairs in horror. Mrs Bant jerked in her chair a few times and then slumped to the floor. I noticed that Fay was holding her head in her hands and the Reverend Marshall was deathly pale.

Suddenly Jack's chair toppled to the floor and him with it, then Mr Bant also fell to the floor.

The Continental voice said loudly, 'Take him out. We must deal with him another way.'

It seemed to me we were surrounded by noise as one would hear in a fight, then suddenly it was gone. I could hear the sound of bitter sobbing coming from the hall and realised the burst of frenzy was over.

The Continental voice spoke then. 'Please remain as you are. I must leave you to tend to our friend. We will be watching over you all until we meet again. Our little lady here will soon recover, but will need time afterwards to regain her strength. God bless you and keep you all.'

Mrs Bant was still on the floor and not moving. I glanced at my watch and was surprised. We had only been in the sitting proper for fifteen minutes at most. Mr Bant went to his wife and was holding her hands in his.

I looked at Jack who was still on the floor and saw that he was as white as a sheet and seemed to be in pain.

'Jack, are you all right?'

He looked at me. 'I think I've sprained my ankle, and my shoulder is hurt.' We found later he had sprained his left ankle and dislocated his shoulder. He was, needless to say, very shaken and slept little for some nights afterwards. As he so aptly put it: 'I've seen some things in the army and been involved in some unpleasant things as soldiers are, but this beats all.'

Fay, I discovered, had been hit by flying ornaments on her cheeks and nose. Fortunately there were no bones broken, but she showed the bruising for many days afterwards and had stitches in her left eyebrow and cheek.

Reverend Marshall remained seated in his chair and just stared in front of him. It was a full ten minutes before we could coax him to speak to us; he seemed to be in a catatonic state. John was trembling and very pale and also concerned about Fay.

Mrs Bant took an age to come to and even then it was some time before she felt she could move and go next door. All the time I could hear the same sobbing, despairing cry in the distance, presumably upstairs.

Mr and Mrs Bant remained with us until late in the evening. It was Mr Bant who drove the Reverend Marshall home, and Fay and Jack to the hospital. He was also very helpful in a practical down-to-earth way. He helped me to make tea and we decided that a strong pick-me-up was needed for the vicar and for John. For Jack and Fay he would allow nothing until they had been to the hospital. Obviously the correct story could not be told to the hospital staff and they concocted a story about injuring themselves while putting up decorations for a party. It was arranged we would all meet again the following Saturday for discussion only. No one felt able to face another sitting so soon. We were assured by Mr and Mrs Bant that their spirit helpers would look after 'him' next door and us also; provided we did not enter the house next door we would be all right.

All had been quiet in our house throughout the night and the next day. I was surprised at this and expected more disturbances to follow our last sitting. It was a bit unnerving to hear nothing at all and the silence was louder than the noise. We sat in the living room in the Olivers' house the next evening, all looking and feeling weary. We had little appetite and wasted more food than we had eaten. I did most of the work and cooking for the day, as I seemed to be least affected by what had happened.

John and Fay dozed off and poor Jack sat with one arm in a sling and a foot securely strapped up and resting on a stool like someone with gout. None of us had clearly stated whether or not we were prepared to return next door for another sitting.

'I suppose Mr and Mrs Bant are used to that sort of thing,' said Jack. 'They must know what to expect and the dangers involved.' Fay looked at Jack.

'I don't know I want to go through all that again. By the look of the Reverend Marshall I wouldn't think he would either,' she said. 'He looked as if he didn't understand what was happening at all and looked positively ghastly when he left here. I'm sure he thinks the haunting is pure evil.' She looked at each of us in turn and then said, 'I can't help feeling sorry for the poor soul who is doing the haunting though, so not to go on would be like leaving a job undone or breaking a promise. There it is, I can't help feeling the way I do, can I?' She looked at her husband. 'I'm sorry, John, that's the way I feel.'

Relief swept over me. I could still count on Fay, she would go on. I felt tears pricking my eyes. I wanted to go on with the sittings to find out what happened in the past to bring about such suffering. Most of all, I wanted to be able to live in my own house.

That 'he' next door needed help I was convinced, and having started we should go on. He must have gone through some very unhappy times to have been brought to this final maniacal state. From what we had heard so far it seemed his only crime was in loving too much where his love was not returned.

I was consumed with curiosity and was determined to find out all I could. Anyway, we couldn't live in that house as things were and I desperately wanted to live there and make it our home, but this I couldn't do yet.

On the following Saturday we all gathered in the sitting room. We were not going into our house for a sitting as no one was really up to it. Fay still showed the facial bruises quite clearly, and where the stitches were her face still looked very sore. John was also very weary. He had been to work through the week but really he would have been better at home. Jack had not been to work and had rested quite a lot, but he still looked very tired. Of all of us I was in best shape. I wanted to get on but I knew I had to be patient.

When Mr and Mrs Bant arrived, they were as cheerful as ever, although they too looked weary.

Fay had prepared tea, which we could eat sitting round the fire. We drew the curtains and sat with the firelight flickering around us. It all looked very cosy and homely.

Mrs Bant looked at me and said, 'Are you going on with it?'

'Oh yes,' I said, not realising I had said it. I knew that Jack and John had doubts and felt that enough was enough, but at least Fay showed willing.

'Of course, you do understand that future sittings could be much worse than anything we have been through so far, don't you?' said Mr Bant. 'The violence could increase and probably will do so. He is going to take a lot of persuading to leave and he may have to be removed by force. The spirit rescuers never like doing that because it does not really help the one who is Earthbound. You see, until we can understand that we have died and can understand the wrongs we have done during our Earth life, we cannot progress in the spirit world.'

'How much more do these spirit rescuers think we can take?' Jack asked, his voice edgy. 'After all, we are not the first couple to be upset and frightened. If that man were alive he would have been removed by now. Why not the same rules here?'

'It doesn't work that way in the spirit world. There, they have to work by certain rules, and one is that those who have done wrong in their Earth life should know they have done wrong. Until they do they won't progress,' replied Mrs Bant.

'Oh, come on,' I said. 'None of us knows what that man has gone through to make him the way he is. Surely he can't be entirely to blame, he must have been driven to it by something.'

'You're quite right,' said Mrs Bant, 'but still, from what he has said, he has enjoyed doing what he has done. We don't know the full story, do we?'

'No, we don't know the full story,' I agreed, 'but it seems to me that his mind has broken. None of us know how much we would be able to take.'

And that was the understatement of the year, as I was to find out at a later date.

The conversation kept circling the whole problem through the evening, until at last I had to ask when we would be going back to try again.

'Not for another month,' said Mr Bant. 'That seems a long time to wait, but it isn't really and it will give more time to those in spirit to do more from their side.'

Chapter Six

I was pleased at the delay. It meant I could spent some time on my research into the background leading up to the present troubles. Jack and I also had to make some arrangements for residence, as I felt it would not be right to stay on with Fay and John indefinitely. However, when we put this to them, they were adamant that we should remain with them.

Fay said, 'The place wouldn't be the same without you.' Then added, 'I feel safer with you here, Laura.'

Tuesday morning found me in the newspaper library looking through old newspapers for the years 1964 to 1965. I intended to go through each one page by page and had armed myself with a notebook and pencil, hoping to find some relevant items.

Time passed swiftly and it was soon lunchtime. I would have loved a cup of tea, but I could not leave what I was doing just yet. I had told Fay I would not be home for lunch, as I wanted to spend the day searching for information.

I had all but lost hope when I came to a small advertisement in one paper dated 10th October, 1964, in the personal column. 'Charlie, waiting for you to come home, Glenda.' But Glenda who? I had no evidence that Glenda was our the wife of our 'lodger', yet I knew I was right.

I copied out the advertisement very carefully and made a note of the date on the newspaper in readiness to begin next day. Then I made my way home, feeling quite jubilant.

When I told the others of my find, they weren't quite so sure I had the right person, although Jack did say, 'If she feels it's right then it must be. I didn't listen before and we all know the result of that.'

Fay and John laughed, but I knew Jack was serious. 'But how can I find her address, and even if I got it, after all this time she may not be still there?' I said.

'Now, now. Faint heart never won fair lady,' said Jack.

'I must be right,' I thought, 'if Jack is so sure I am.'

The telephone rang, making us all jump. Fay answered it and came back into the room looking quite puzzled.

'It was a lady on the phone,' she said. 'She says she read about your troubles in the newspaper some weeks ago, but felt too embarrassed to contact us before. Anyway, she feels she can help but she wouldn't say how. She is coming over tonight.'

'It's her,' I said, not knowing how I knew. 'Heavens, what time will she arrive? It's half past seven now.'

'Oh, she said about nine,' said Fay. 'Do you really think it's her?'

'If it isn't, then it's someone connected with her,' I said. 'I'm sure I'm right.'

Sure enough, at nine o'clock there was a ring at the doorbell. I went to answer it. She was a small sharp-faced woman in her early forties. I brought her into the room and introduced her to everyone. I then realised I didn't know her name.

'I'm Monica Preston,' she said. 'I'm sorry to barge in like this, but I am sure I can help you, or rather, we can help each other.'

I wasn't sure I liked her, but still I had to be polite, especially as I was in someone else's home.

'How can we help each other?' I asked her.

'Well,' she said, 'it's like this. My brother lived next door to here until he died. His wife had left him, you know. He never was much of a go-getter and such a temper he had. Anyway, she, his wife I mean, left him for another man; not that I blame her the way he made her suffer; but one day he, the boyfriend that is, went out and didn't come back.'

She settled in the armchair, lighting a cigarette. 'Glenda, my sister-in-law, kept in touch with me until she killed herself about two years after Harry, my brother, her husband, you know. She killed herself just like Harry, queer that, the two of them. I've got their children, you know, there being no one else to look after them. Three there are, and terrors they are too.'

'Mrs Preston, how does this help us, or you?' I asked.

'Well, it's this way you see.' She sat there blowing smoke around like a fog.

A ferret, I thought, and just as dangerous too if crossed.

She went on, 'The last child my sister-in-law had was Charlie's, that's the boyfriend. I'd like to get in touch with him to get him to pay something towards his child's keep. Fancy disappearing like that. Not a word to anyone, just went, he did. She wasn't very lucky with the men in her life it seems to me.'

'What makes you think we know where Charlie is?' asked John.

'Well, you see, it was like this. My brother was locked up for years for some terrible crimes, but one day he escaped. There was a lot of publicity but they never got him. Soon after that, Charlie disappeared. I've often wondered if the two were connected. Perhaps Harry frightened him off, he was mad enough to, mad, mad I mean, not angry. So I wondered when Harry came back here if he'd seen any of the neighbours, whether he'd said anything to anyone. After all, Charlie ought to pay something for his kid, didn't he?'

'I'm afraid we can't help you,' said Fay. 'We have only lived here for six years and we never discuss our neighbours with anybody.' She got up to open the door and I knew she disliked our visitor as much as I did.

'Oh well, I'm sorry you've been troubled,' said Mrs Preston. 'If you do hear anything, you'll let me know, won't you?'

'I really don't think we will,' said Fay. 'We don't make a habit of discussing other people's personal problems.'

'Mrs Preston,' I said, 'before you go, what was Charlie's surname, just in case we do hear anything, and would you give me your address?'

'Oh, Lambert,' she said with a sickly smile. 'Charlie Lambert. Thank you ever so much. If you hear anything, my address is 21 Filbert Terrace, just off the High Road. Cheerio, everyone.'

'Well,' exploded Jack when she had gone. 'What a vicious, crawling woman. That poor man next door. With a nagging wife and a sister like that I don't wonder his mind cracked. You surely wouldn't tell her anything, would you?' he asked me.

'Of course not,' I replied. 'Anyway, we know Charlie's dead, don't we, but we can't prove it as yet.'

Chapter Seven

The next day was overcast and chilly. I told Fay I would be going back to the library again, which she understood.

'We're back to square one,' she said. 'My hopes were soaring, but all that woman wanted was for us to help her get money from this Charlie. Still, I expect it does take money to bring up a family these days.'

'She was a bit blatant though, wasn't she?' I said. 'I wouldn't have had the nerve to put it so bluntly, would you?'

Fay grinned. 'Indeed not, but then she did say she was too embarrassed to call us before last night.'

She looked as if she was in doubt about what to say next.

'Out with it, Fay, what are you thinking about?' I said, laughing. 'There is definitely something on your mind.'

Fay's eyes met mine, and they looked very serious. 'I just feel we haven't heard the last of Monica Preston,' she said. 'I'm sure she is going to cause trouble somehow, somewhere, and we had better be careful or it will rub off on us.'

'You didn't like her either then. You certainly made haste to the door when she seemed ready to go.'

'Like her!' exclaimed Fay. 'I detested her from the first moment I set eyes on her. She's a wolf in sheep's clothing, of that I am sure. Do be careful of her, Laura.'

I looked at her. 'I will, Fay. Still, I'm glad no one said anything about our sittings with the Bants to her. I don't think any of us cared for her at all.'

There being nothing else left to say, I took myself off to the library again. I decided to backtrack through September 1964 and then work forward from there. I found what I was looking for in an issue dated 24th September in the Stop Press section. '*Man found dead in house. Married couple find body in their house when they return from honeymoon.*'

The next information, in an issue dated two weeks later, gave more details. It gave the address where the dead man was found, which was our house.

The report said that he had killed himself while the balance of his mind was disturbed. It gave his name as Mr Harold Carpenter, aged forty-six years, and said that he had escaped from a secure prison a few weeks before the date of his death.

Making a copy of all this and the date of the newspapers, I went, in some jubilation, to report my findings to Fay.

She met me at the front door as I went in. 'You look pleased with yourself, like a cat who's been at the cream.'

'Oh Fay, look what I've got.' I dragged her into the sitting room excitedly. 'It all ties up with what he told us. Come and look before I burst.'

I took the notebook out of my bag and laid my prized information on the table. Fay read it through. 'Well, I'm blessed,' she said. 'Wait 'til the men see this.'

Jack had returned to work. Both he and John looked weary, and I suspected that John wasn't sleeping any better than Jack.

'Fay, I wish you'd join me at the library, it would be so much quicker with the two of us, and we could double check what we think we find if we both went.'

She said, 'I think I will. I feel safer near you somehow. I know it doesn't make sense but I feel if I stay with you I'll be all right. Silly of me, isn't it?'

I looked at her closely and realised how tired and worried she felt.

'Has anything happened today?' I asked.

'Oh, there has been a great deal of noise. I'm afraid your furniture must be suffering very badly by now, Laura. I know it's pessimistic, but I have the feeling something awful is going to happen. The sooner we can get this over and done with, the better. We've still to wait three weeks before we have another sitting. I just feel we're sitting on dynamite.'

'Fay, listen. I've been wondering whether to go to the police to see if they will send someone round when we have the next sitting, in plain clothes of course. We might find out where he has put Charlie Lambert. The police could take it from there, couldn't they?'

'Well, I think you should check with Mr and Mrs Bant about that, Laura. It depends on them.'

'But Fay, suppose we are told where Charlie's body is, how do we tell the police then?' I queried.

'See if Mr and Mrs Bant agree first,' she said. 'I only hope the vicar will still come. It lends credence to our story for the police if he does.'

I hugged her. 'Fay, you're marvellous. I wouldn't have thought of that.'

When John and Jack came home, we told them what I had found and asked what they thought about bringing the police in. They both agreed with Fay that we should contact the Bants before doing anything.

I telephoned Mr and Mrs Bant, but before agreeing to anything they said they would discuss it first with us. We arranged that they should visit the evening of Friday of the next week, staying over the weekend at a local hotel.

Fay and I spent all the time we could in the library, but by the time Friday came we had found nothing further, except a small report stating that Charles Lambert had been missing from home since 18th September, 1964. This I carefully copied out in my notebook.

We didn't go out at all on Friday, and waited with impatience and some trepidation for the Bants to arrive in the evening.

When Mr and Mrs Bant saw the information I had copied from the newspaper, they were very impressed.

'Everything seems to fit,' said Mrs Bant.

'It never ceases to amaze me how the truth of what is given to us from the spirit world can be proved even though the recipient may be quite unaware of the facts. I know this is somewhat different, but the same principle applies.'

'Yes, this is true,' joined in Mr Bant. 'Very often those receiving messages have to go to others in the family to find out the truth of a spirit message. To many the messages may be utterly trivial, but to the person concerned the message is proof that their loved ones still live. There just is no death, and we cannot help but accept it as fact. It took my wife and I some time to accept. We first went to a meeting out of curiosity and for a bit of a laugh, but because of the evidence we were given we had no cause to treat it all as a joke.'

'What about asking the police to come to the next sitting?' I asked.

They looked at one another and Mr Bant replied, 'Well, it is a good idea, and if they would agree to send someone along it would be marvellous. It could clear up at least one police file on missing persons. The trouble is, a lot of them think we are cranks and don't take this seriously at all. Very few think we are credible, but they are not alone in this. Anyway, it is worth a try. It will have to be someone who will understand, or at least try to, but the next sitting will not be an easy one at all. Perhaps we could go along to see them next Saturday morning. Would that suit you?'

'Oh yes,' I said, 'that would be fine.' I must confess I felt some joy that they had agreed so easily. I thought it would be a matter of making a simple request for an officer to attend, but nothing is ever simple, as I was to discover.

Fay said, 'I hope the vicar will still come, but he's not a young man, and may find it a bit much.'

Mr Bant smiled at her. 'It is a strain, and as you say he is not young. You must not be disappointed if he drops out, and also if the police don't take us seriously. This is one of the most difficult cases my wife and I have been on, and the next sitting may well be more violent. In any case, we are not sitting for another two weeks so we can all get plenty of rest in the meantime. Whatever you do, don't go back into the house. Avoid any unnecessary stress. We'll be here next Saturday morning, but don't build your hopes too high.'

The rest of the evening passed very pleasantly in general conversation, and they left at about nine o'clock.

I decided not to go back to the library again until after our next sitting. I did not think I could get much more relevant information. All we had to do now was to wait for the next week to pass.

The following Monday morning I telephoned the local police station to make an appointment for the following Saturday to speak to the chief officer in charge. I had to give a reason for the request, and the only answer I could give was that it concerned a murder enquiry. I had to explain that it could not be before Saturday as all the persons who would be coming could not attend before then. The officer who spoke to me sounded very dubious but said he would try to arrange an interview, asked me for my name, address and telephone number and said he would contact me as soon as possible. This he did the same afternoon, and said that a Chief Inspector Barbrum would see us at 11 a.m. the following Saturday morning.

I telephoned Mr and Mrs Bant to confirm that they would be able to attend the interview with us with Chief Inspector Barbrum, and asked them to bring the tapes and tape recorder with them in case they were needed. There matters had to stand for the rest of the week.

We heard much noise on two occasions coming from our house and I wondered if anything at all would be left that we could use.

Jack was still having a lot of pain, and he and John were not sleeping at all well. They kept saying that nothing they had been through in the armed forces had prepared them for this. Fay and I seemed the most calm of all of us. It was very difficult hearing all the racket coming from our house and not being able to check on the damage. I was quite sure that when everything was over we would need to replace or have restored most of our furniture. It is a good thing not to be able to see into the future, for had I been able to, I doubt if I would have continued.

Fay and I worked hard through the week cleaning and washing and preparing food for the freezer so that there would be as little do to as possible from Saturday for at least a few days.

Forewarned is forearmed and in a way I think we must have been.

Chapter Eight

At last Saturday came and Fay, John, Jack and I with Mr and Mrs Bant duly presented ourselves at the police station. We did not have long to wait before we were led into the office of Chief Inspector Barbrum.

He was a tall, well-built man with hair just starting to go grey. His eyes were a piercing blue and his eyelashes were almost babyish they were so long. I judged his age to be about forty-five years.

Babyish his eyelashes might have been, but I discovered he was a very strong-minded and dedicated police officer. It seemed to me he would need much convincing just to listen to us. I could not blame him for that, though, as I am sure his workload must have been very heavy.

He looked at us with raised eyebrows as we all trooped into his office, and no doubt thought we were some kind of deputation from a 'bring back hanging' group or something similar.

There were not sufficient chairs for us all to sit, and seeing this, the chief inspector strode over to the door, opened it and shouted to another officer to bring in four more chairs. When these had been brought in he told us all to sit down, and sat looking at us each in turn.

'Well,' he said, 'what can I do for you?'

I sat there feeling uncomfortable and wondered how I was going to explain everything in a way he would understand. However, I felt that someone had to say something so I thought that I had better start to explain.

Taking my courage in both hands, I said, 'It is a bit difficult to explain, Chief Inspector, but when you hear what we have to tell you I hope you will not feel we have wasted your time.'

'I'll be the judge of that,' he replied. 'Just tell me from the beginning all you know.'

Ouch, I thought, a bad start. Anyway, I had to say something so I started explaining.

'Well, you see, when you hear what we have discovered, and how, you may think we are just a lot of cranky people.' I took a breath and continued. 'My husband and I bought a house and all was fine for a while. Then, without warning, we had a very frightening experience.' I went on to tell him about that first dreadful night, and all the subsequent events. I'd brought my notebook with me, and showed him the notes I'd made. He just sat and looked at me with those piercing blue eyes.

I thought it time I introduced Fay and John, and told him of the way they had helped us, and that we were still living with them. Then I introduced Mr and Mrs Bant, and told him how they had come into the picture. Also of the visit by Monica Preston, who I felt was not to be trusted, but I didn't know why I felt like that.

The chief inspector turned to Mr Bant and asked, 'Explain your part in all this.'

Mr Bant explained as best he could about belonging to a rescue circle, and told the chief inspector they had taped recordings of the sittings in our house. 'You may find it difficult to understand, regarding our work, and most people think we are very odd, but our work means a lot to us. What we have on the tapes certainly indicates that a murder was committed back in 1964, but we have at this point in time no idea where the body was left. I must point out though that where Mr and Mrs Gordon live has suffered a lot of damage through psychic phenomena during the time we spent there, short as it was, and subsequently. My wife is a trance medium and works through trance to rescue what we call earthbound spirits, by that I mean people who have died but have not left their place of dwelling or where they were killed. I know it all sounds unbelievable, but what Mrs Gordon has told you is the truth, and in the sittings to try to free the earthbound spirit, both Mr Gordon and Mrs Oliver sustained injuries. The sittings were very violent and if repeated could get even more so.' He paused, and the piercing blue eyes remained fixed on him.

Mr Bant continued, 'My wife and I have brought the tapes and a recorder so that you can hear for yourself what took place. You must understand that we cannot prove a murder occurred, but I would say that it undoubtedly did.'

Chief Inspector Barbrum got up from his chair and went to the window looking out on the street below for a few minutes. We all sat completely still in our chairs not daring to move.

Suddenly he swung round. 'Right,' he said, 'let's hear the tapes you've brought. There's a plug over here you can use.'

Mr Bant plugged in and set the first tape recording working. All was silent in the room except for the sound of the tape recording. When that had finished he set the next one working, and after that the third and final one.

When they had all been played through, Chief Inspector Barbrum looked from one to the other of us.

'When do you plan to have another 'sitting', as you call it? I'd like to be there, but I must talk to the chief superintendent about this first. Dead men don't usually talk, as you might say, but I must admit it intrigues me. I've never heard anything like it before, and probably never will again.' The chief inspector swung round to me. 'Then again, if this is a hoax, you could all find yourselves in a lot of trouble for wasting police time. First, I would have to find out if there is anything on the files concerning all this and I'm sure you are aware that murder enquiries take a lot of time and effort. We've got better things to do than run around after hoax and nonsense reports.'

I felt his eyes were boring holes right through me, but then anger came to the fore. 'Chief Inspector, all my husband and I want is to live in our house in peace and quiet, not in fear. In any case, we cannot live there as things are. Not only is it horrifying and terrifying, but downright dangerous.'

'All right, Laura,' said Jack, putting his hand over mine, 'don't get yourself worked up. I told you we'll sell the place, that's if we can get anyone to buy it, of course. We don't ever have to go back there ever again, you know that.'

'Inspector,' Fay butted in, 'we have lived next door to that house for six years and every time a family has moved in they have just as quickly moved out again. The noise of furniture and crockery being smashed about is unbelievable. Only when the house is empty is everything quiet. By empty I mean no one living there, no furniture – really empty. They really are not playing about or wasting your time. My husband and I were at those sittings, and I have never been so terrified in my life.'

Chief Inspector Barbrum looked at Mr and Mrs Bant. 'Well, when are you going back there?'

Mrs Bant looked at him and then at her husband. 'We planned to go back one week from today. We do not play at what we do, it is much too dangerous. During the sittings I am in a trance state, and know nothing of what occurs until afterwards, when I hear the recording. Our work, particularly for me, is very demanding, both physically and mentally, and when we have finished this work period I shall need at least eight weeks to really get strong again. You must also know and really understand that if you or any other police officer joins us in the sitting you must be in plain clothes and you must be prepared for violence. Not the kind of violence you can deal with physically as you would restrain a disturbed and violent prisoner, no, this would be a murderer you could never take hold of, never get into court, and never get to sign a statement. You have to know what you are getting into before you get any police officer involved, because the risk of injury is great, the man is so disturbed mentally. I am hoping my spirit guides and helpers will have been able to calm him by the time Saturday comes, but I cannot tell what the outcome will be. Don't walk into this without realising the dangers; they are great.'

'Would you all be prepared to make statements concerning this?' we were asked, and in one voice said, 'Yes.'

'Well then,' he said, 'that's what we will have from each of you, and also, can I keep the tapes for the chief superintendent to hear?'

'Yes,' said Mr Bant. 'We have made copies of all of them. Can we ask, please, that none of this is leaked to the press, because if reporters came around the house at the time of the sitting, the situation would become more dangerous.'

'Very well, I will make sure the press are kept out of it,' said the chief inspector, 'but I will not be able to do anything on this without the chief superintendent's agreeing. You will have to wait to hear from me, and that will be during next week sometime. I will phone Mr Oliver's house to confirm, or otherwise, police involvement.'

He then arranged for us to give our statements in his presence, alone, and when we had all completed these and signed them we were allowed home.

What we all needed was a cup of tea when we arrived back at Fay and John's house. We sat round the fire not saying much while we drank it. I think we all felt drained and exhausted. There was nothing more we could do but await the chief inspector's call.

Part Two

Chapter Nine

1930–1946

Monica lay curled up in total misery on her bed. Her back hurt so much where her mother had caned her, that she couldn't lie on it. Sobs shook her little body, and the hatred for her brother consumed her. Why do I always have to be blamed for what he does? Mum only thinks of him and he knows he can wrap her round his little finger. Oh, I hate him, hate him, he's a horrible little sod.

As far back as she could remember she had taken the beatings that little beast deserved. There was the time a neighbour had come to the house carrying a dead cat. He said he had seen Harry kicking it, and when he'd collared him he'd run away.

'I'll swing for your boy one of these days,' he'd shouted, but Mum had shouted back at him, 'Clear off, my Harry wouldn't do anything like that, you daft bugger.' Then she'd slammed the door. Harry had come in through the back door into the kitchen. On his face was a smile so angelic no one would believe him capable of such acts.

Mum had grabbed her, Monica, by the hair, and slapped her one way and then the other across the face.

'What do you mean by letting your brother get into trouble? You're supposed to look after him.' Still holding her by the hair, she had reached for the cane and belaboured her across the back. 'That'll teach you to do as

you're told, you silly little sod. You stay with him in future.
I don't want no more trouble with neighbours. Now get to
your bed, and you'll have no tea neither. Go and get up
them stairs.'

As Monica stumbled toward the staircase door she saw
the smile on Harry's face widen, and then heard him laugh.
She daren't say anything or she would get another welting,
but oh, how she hated him. She lay curled up on her bed
and it seemed to her that she was always getting a caning
from her mother for something Harry had done. He'd
either punched little girls, or kicked cats and puppies,
sometimes to death. It just wasn't fair. He wouldn't stay
with her anyway, however much she tried to make him.
Off he'd go, and when he came back a while later there was
always a satisfied grin on his face, and seeing that grin,
Monica knew he'd been up to something and she would
probably be belted for it.

She heard Mum saying to Harry after she'd been sent to
bed, 'Don't you take on, never mind about them people.
You can do as you like, boy, as long as you're happy.'
Whatever people said he'd done, Mum never believed
them. 'No one's going to touch you, my boy, Mum will see
to that.'

Monica was ten years old, and already her back was
showing scars from frequent canings. It was no good saying
anything to her Dad, he was just like Mum except that he
would belt Harry, and Monica enjoyed seeing that. When
that happened, the grin on Harry's face changed. Oh, how
he cried for Mum then. After that there would be a ding-
dong of a row between Mum and Dad, with Mum ending
up with a black eye or a split lip. Monica liked to see that
too. Bit of my own back without having to do anything, she
would think.

One day, when Monica was fourteen years old, someone came to the door to tell Mum that Dad had had an accident at work, and had been taken to hospital. Monica was at work by now in a factory a few roads away, so she didn't learn about this until she came home late in the evening. Mum was sitting in the kitchen, her face grim.

'Your dad's dead,' she said bluntly, 'killed today at work. Don't look like we'll have any money coming in but yours, and my bit from cleaning, so we'll have to really pull our horns in.'

'Why can't Harry get a paper boy's job, or delivering groceries to help out? I had to at his age.'

Before she could move, her mother was out of her chair, and her hand had smacked Monica across the face, her face red with anger.

'My boy, work like any common boy round here? Never. We'll keep him until he's old enough to go out to work himself. Why should he suffer? You're a selfish piece, my girl, and that's a fact.'

When she had a day off, Monica would watch Harry enjoying himself in the garden, such as it was. He had a number of wire cages and would catch wild birds, put them in the cages and watch with pleasure as they threw themselves against the wire, eventually breaking their wings. Then he would sit silently, on his face a broad grin, while they slowly died. He sickened her, but it was no good saying anything, for that ended up in another belting for herself.

'What's up with you, you daft bitch, they're only birds. As long as he's happy, what's it matter?'

Harry found he could really do as he liked to anyone or anything, as long as he got away quickly, before he was spotted by someone. Little girls in the park. He enjoyed knocking them about, the younger the better. Then the cats and dogs. If there was no one near he would use them like a football, always running as soon as someone appeared to find out why the little creatures were mewing or yelping. He'd run away, laughing fit to burst. It made him feel good. He'd joined up with a gang of youths who went looking for trouble, getting into fights, but as he always got a beating, being quite small, he gave that up. Mum would always get so worked up when he went home with a bloody nose, her fussing got on his nerves in the end. No, it was better to do things that made him feel good when he was on his own.

As he got older he stayed out later and later, long after darkness fell. If he saw an old man or old woman walking alone he'd creep up behind them, give them a good push so that they fell over, kick them a couple of times, and then run away laughing. He liked that game but he made sure no one else was around when he did it. He had nearly got caught once and he wouldn't make that mistake again.

Even though he grew in years, he did not grow very much in body size. Always slim and not tall. He knew he would be good-looking when he was a man and that pleased him. Oh, he'd make sure that nothing altered his good looks. Didn't get them from Dad that was for sure, great big fat thing he was. Must be from his mum, she was small and slim. He enjoyed fooling his mum, she could never see any wrong in him and he made sure it continued that way. When he eventually started work in the engineering factory, he collected his wages each week and on the way home always bought her a little something, might be a bar of chocolate, cheap bottle of scent, but always something. That kept her sweet. He didn't have to pay any money for his keep, because, as Mum said, 'A boy needs his money to enjoy himself.' So he did. The cinema and clothes were his main enjoyment, apart from when he could use his fists and boots on someone or something. That was the best pleasure of all. Had to be careful though. Had to be sure there was no one around.

That daft sister of his, he could still get her a good welting when he worked it out properly. He took a few shillings from Mum's purse one day, knowing that his sister had bought a pair of stockings. Mum, of course, thought she'd bought them with the money he'd taken. Oh, he'd enjoyed that, such a black eye Monica had. Taking a cake his mother made was another way. He only had to deny it, putting on his angelic face while he did so, and Monica would be for it. Yes, he had Monica right where he wanted her – smashing, it was.

That is what Harry thought, but he was wrong. Monica was determined to leave home, come hell or high water. She had to wait until she'd saved a few shillings though, to keep her going until she'd found a place to live and another job, and nothing, but nothing, would get her back home once she'd left.

She'd also realised that her body could be a useful asset, but she wasn't ready for that yet. She'd have to think more about that one. Men were daft where women were concerned, and when she moved out she intended to make use of her body to get the things she wanted in life. She wouldn't be a common prostitute though. Oh no, she'd be very selective. That was in the future though. One thing she was sure of, she would never marry. She'd never, never, never be the punchbag for any man. When she went to bed with a man, it would be her who would lead the way, and decide when and where.

Every week she saved what little she could by walking to work, or going without tea at break time, or anything else she could save on. She'd got a post office savings book which she kept in her handbag and she never let it out of her sight, even when she got belted by Mum. She would take out the savings book and gloat over the amount as the shillings built up. A long way to go though. She'd had two pay rises by the time she was sixteen, but she told Mum she'd only got half of what she really got. She won't take it all like everything else to give to that rotten little sod of a brother, she thought.

When she was nearly eighteen years old, the war was being threatened in Europe. It was 1938. A lot had happened in recent years. The death of the old king, the abdication of the new one (Daft sod, thought Monica), and the coronation of the new king, King George VI. Well, they can all look after themselves; me, I'm going to look after me. Number one always, I'll be. I'll never have anyone telling me what to do or not to do, no way.

On her eighteenth birthday, she waited until she was alone in the house – she was supposed to be working late – went into the kitchen, picked up a carrier bag and packed her meagre supply of clothes into it. As it was late autumn at least she didn't have to worry about carrying her coat, her one and only coat. Out through the door she went, and along the alleyway into the next street. Catching a bus, she made her way south of the Thames. I'll find a room, doesn't matter how scrubby, then I'll look for a job. Hope I never see them again, they can enjoy each other. He'll have to pay a bit into the housekeeping now, and about time too. She was smiling to herself as she thought of the uproar when they found she'd left. Wish I was a fly on the wall.

In fact, it wasn't until the following night that she was discovered to have left home. Her mother went frantic to find she would not have Monica's money coming in.

'The rotten little bitch, wait 'til I get my hands on her, I'll give her what for. How does she think we're going to eat this week?'

Harry sat eating his dinner, not caring one way or the other. So Monica had left home, so what! Daft sod, he thought. He soon came down to earth when his mother said, 'Well, boy, I'm sorry, but you're going to have to pay me some of your wages, or I'll have nuffink to buy grub with.'

Harry shot out of his chair. 'Why the bloody hell should I? I've never had to before. You go out and earn more money – it's your job to look after me.'

'I know that, lovey boy, and I will get more jobs, but it still won't be enough to keep us, what with the rent and all.'

'You go to hell,' Harry said.

'Well, it's like this, boy,' said his mother. 'You're the man of the house now, and the man of the house has to bring money in. It's the woman's job to pleasure a man, that's what she's here for, but it's the man's job to keep the home going. Because of that rotten little sod, Monica, you've had to grow up before your time. You ain't got no dad, so you're the man of the house.'

'Bloody rotten, I call it!' shouted Harry, as he slammed out of the back door. He walked along the road, rage boiling up within him. The streets were dark, but it was too early in the evening to be able to vent his anger on someone, because there were too many people about. Still, he thought, if I've got to pay housekeeping money and be the man of the house, I'll have my say in things. Mum will let me do what I want – she always has, anyway. She can't argue with the man of the house. He walked around the streets for what seemed like hours, until there were very few people about, rage and self-pity and triumph swelling within him, until he thought he would burst. Then his chance came, just what he'd been waiting for.

An old lady, walking along with a stick, was ahead of him. He sprinted silently towards her, and as she tottered to face him, he pushed her in the face, knocking her to the ground, and as she lay there he kicked her five or six times, wherever his boot could find a place to land, and ran off laughing down the road. Hearing her moaning behind him, he thought he would burst with happiness. Round corners and into alleyways he dodged until he knew he was safe. He walked quietly back home, feeling at peace with himself.

He found his mum still sitting in the kitchen, smiled his angelic smile and said, 'Right, Mum, we're in this together, but if I'm to be the man of the house, things have to be done my way from now on.'

''Course, my boy,' replied his mother. 'How else would it be?'

In the meantime, Monica had found herself a dilapidated room in a slummy area of Stockwell. That didn't matter though, because she wouldn't be staying there. When she'd fixed herself up with a job, she'd get something better. At least it's better than being back home with them. No one's going to belt me around in future.

What few people realised, including Harry, Monica, and their mother, was that a terrible war was looming on the horizon, in which all Europe would suffer.

Chapter Ten

Monica crawled out of bed at five o'clock. Wish the bleeding cows would learn to sleep late. Getting herself washed and dressed, still half asleep, she went down to the farm kitchen for a cup of tea. She hadn't spoken to the other three girls she shared the room with, and they knew better than to speak to her at that time of the morning. Monica drank her tea and made her way out to the cowshed to get everything ready for milking. Still, I had a good time last night. You can do what you like with these Yanks, they'll give you anything for a bit of you-know-what. She smiled to herself, thinking of the nylons and chocolate she'd got stored in the bedroom. And they'll give you some cash too. Hope this war goes on for a long time. She gloated over the thought of the money in her bank book. There was a few hundred pounds stashed away.

Nearby was a USA Air Force camp, and they were mostly here today, and gone tomorrow. Daft sods, she thought. Getting themselves killed. They should be more careful.

She was in the land army, and it was by now February 1944. There were days when the GIs were confined to barracks, and that annoyed Monica. Her evenings off were spent going to dances or the cinema, or best of all in some quiet place away from everyone. She always made arrangements for the latter times a few evenings before, and

made sure that some nice gift or money was forthcoming
before she gave in to whatever young man she was with. A
few had made the mistake of thinking they could get away
with it without payment of some kind, but they then found
before them a tigress ready to use fingernails, fists or her
knees in the right place. The word went round that she was
an easy touch, but she always made sure they made it worth
her while. Well, I'm doing them a service really, she'd think
to herself. Right tight their feelings would be, tight like
elastic stretched, but I won't do it for nothing, and not with
just anybody neither.

Some of the GIs looked at her as if she was dirt, but that
didn't bother Monica. They're just jealous, Monica would
think. Wouldn't have them touch me anyway.

She had little to do with the other three land army girls
on the farm, she didn't want anyone queering her pitch.
Anyway, they were so namby-pamby they made you laugh.
They could have a good time too, if they weren't so goody
goody.

However late she stayed out, and getting in late was
sometimes a problem, but she'd got the farmer's young son
thinking she was someone special, she was never late for
work. The farmer could hardly complain because she made
sure she did her job well.

By now she was twenty-four years old and made sure
she made the most of her looks. She'd changed her hair to
blonde, using peroxide, and as soon as she had done that
she found a new world opened out for her. Men really *do*
prefer blondes. What a daft lot men are, she thought. With
her dark eyebrows and heavily mascara'd eyes she turned
many heads, and enjoyed every minute of it.

Twice she'd thought she could be in love, but then,
remembering her mother's life, which seemed no different

from any other woman's along the road, she soon squashed those thoughts in her mind. I'll never marry. Never will I play second fiddle to any man or anyone else.

Meanwhile, Harry was enjoying himself too. He was now a sergeant, and could throw his weight around with the men and they couldn't hit back. He thought that was great. He revelled in the bloodshed, and seeing hurt or dead men, or women, gave him a thrill. Not that he showed his feelings, that would never do, people might start asking questions. He had to pretend he was shocked at the sights he saw, but when alone he hugged the memories to him and relived what he had seen, piece by piece. Oh, the sight of blood was lovely, smashing colour blood was.

Harry had made sure he had risen in the ranks as quickly as possible. His lust for power over others burned inside him. He knew he was the most unpopular sergeant on the camp. Already he had been abroad, but was sent home with a leg wound. That was awful, because he couldn't get away from the other men. For the nurses he had no time at all. Simpering lot, he thought. Must think they've all got bloody wings.

After a period at home with his mum, he had been sent to this camp. Oh, how Mum had fussed. Quite made him sick it did, but he put on his angelic smile and got anything he wanted. Black market eggs and bacon, anything his mum could lay her hands on for him. She worked in a factory canteen now, and many bits came home tucked away in her clothes or wherever else she could hide it. Harry didn't care as long as he got it.

There was devastation all over the East End of London, especially near the docks. Although houses in the street where they lived had been razed to the ground, their house still stood firm with the two either side of theirs.

By now, people were feeling the effect of the food rationing. The rations allowed just about enough to feed them, but no extras, so the black marketers did a roaring trade. Good for them, wish I was in it too, thought Harry. I'd black a few eyes to get what I want.

Being in the army had taught Harry a degree of self-defence, and he didn't mind getting into a fight now and again, but he made sure they were men of his own size, not big men. Still, being a sergeant you could throw your weight around and the men would have to obey. Harry liked that, and he'd see it continued when he got back to Civvy Street.

As 1944 continued toward the summer, there seemed to be a lot of troop convoys all heading south. Everyone started wondering what was to happen. On 6th June the skies over the south of England were filled with the droning of aircraft. It seemed the whole sky was filled with them.

Troop ships moved out of harbour from the south of the country and headed toward France. The big day, D-Day, was here. Harry was aboard one of the ships and heading toward the fighting. Bloody hell, back again, he thought. Have to make sure I won't cop another lot. Nevertheless the thought of all the carnage to come excited him. He'd see blood, lots of lovely blood. Great, providing it's not mine. Oh, Harry would be very careful indeed.

Chapter Eleven

When Monica had joined the land army, she had had to give her mother's name and address to the authorities as her next of kin, not that she ever worried about that. She never went to see her mother, and she didn't even think about her.

The flying bomb, pilotless aircraft, had caused more damage as though the London blitz had not been enough. Other cities, such as Coventry and Portsmouth, had been bombed heavily with many civilian casualties, men, women, and children. Those who were not killed, were maimed for life. People would hear the flying bomb, which was officially called the V-1, wait for the engine to stop, then watch it circling round until suddenly it would plummet to the ground. There was a fascination in watching it, but all prayed it would not fall where they were.

However, worse was to come: the V-2, a rocket which would be fired from France or Belgium, and if you happened to be where it fell, you heard no more, for you would be dead, but for those who were not on that particular spot, the blast would cause grave injuries, and many buildings suffered blast damage. To many people, these were worse than all the other bombs, but they came to think, If my number is on it, that's my lot anyway.

Monica never cared about this carnage. She was far away from it all and enjoying herself. She was, therefore, surprised one day to receive an official letter telling her that her mother had been killed by a V-2 rocket. Silly sod, she thought. Fancy getting in the way of one of those. It didn't enter her head that it was not possible to 'get out of the way' of this type of bomb, but, ever ready for the main chance, she immediately wrote to the landlord to ask if she could rent the house her mother had lived in. That'll be a place of my own to go back to when this lot is over, and that's what I'll need. Anyway, got to get in before that rotten brother of mine. If I have the rent book in my name I can kick him out in the street when he comes home. Serve him right after all I've suffered for him.

So Monica became the tenant of the house in which she was born. She was seldom there, but paid three months' rent always in advance so that she could be sure the house was always there when she wanted it.

She started travelling to London, sorting through the furniture, such as it was. When this lot's over I'll get all this changed when I can, she thought. She got the locks changed and made sure that she left nothing of any value there.

At least she had a place to take any men friends to if she fancied doing so, which was not often, and she made sure it was worth her while to do so. Her bank book showed a larger balance as the weeks and months crept on, until at last the war was over in Europe.

Monica eventually left the land army and lived permanently at home. She gave no thought to the sufferings of the many in Europe and the concentration camps. Her one and only thought was how to look after number one, herself.

I've got enough in my bank to live on for a while until I get a decent job. There'll be no slave-driving job for me ever again. Won't need to, the life I intend to live. My slaving days are over. Reckon with my looks I ought to do all right.

As she walked around the East End of London and saw the devastation, she decided the best place for her was 'up west'. So to the West End of London she made her way, looking for work. Got to get a job where I can look smart all the time, posh my voice up a bit, and I reckon I'll do all right.

She got work eventually in a large department store. The floor manager liked the look of her. She carried herself well and dressed well. Ladies fashions, not that there was much to sell. Most polite she was to customers and to the staff. What she said to herself about them they never knew. 'Charming' they all thought her, and how she laughed to herself when alone.

Within three years she was the floor manager of her own department. She made sure she was always very smartly dressed, her hair beautifully styled, and ran her department with a rod of iron.

In the course of her work she met many men who took a great fancy to her. That many were married she cared not. As long as they gave her what she wanted, money, clothes, jewellery, and most of all a good time, she was prepared to give herself. So her life continued. The only black area in her round of enjoyment was when Harry returned from the army. She discovered that her mother had saved for years just to give Harry some money 'should anything happen' to her.

The old cow, always him first, never even thought of me.

Still, Monica got her own back by telling him 'to clear off' when he came to the house. She was the tenant and no way was he going to live with her.

'If you try it again, I'll get the police to clear you out. You go and find your own place to live, sod off.' So saying, she slammed the door in his face.

Harry too had saved some money. After all, who needed money to get what he wanted and needed? A packet of cigarettes, or a bit of food from the stores was all he needed. So grateful everyone had been to those who had freed them from the German jackboot. Even in Germany where they were starving, he'd been able to get rid of the tension within. He'd made sure he would never be found out, of course. His twisted, secretive mind was well able to get over those problems.

On his way home he met a quiet and meek young ATS girl, and he cultivated her friendship. He'd learned she had no family, so there would be no irate father around to speak up for her. Oh, he played his cards well. Settling her in a room near his home, he'd gone off well pleased with himself. The shock came when Monica opened the door, but instead of making him welcome she'd made it clear he wasn't going to live off her or with her. Raging, he went down the road. Have to think about this. That Glenda will do anything I ask, got her in the palm of my hand. Have to go careful though, mustn't scare her off. Have to marry her, then I'll have someone at my beck and call for good. His demob suit didn't feel right after the army uniform he'd worn for so long. Job first, he thought, and headed towards the factory he'd worked at before.

On his way, he saw a house for sale down a quiet street, right at the far end of a cul-de-sac. 'For Sale' the board said. Might as well see what they want for it. He thought the price a bit steep but with bargaining got it down two hundred pounds. Can manage that, what with what I've saved, and Mum's money, and I expect Glenda's saved a bit. Borrow the rest, then we can settle in.

Things did work out right for Harry. Glenda had saved a bit, so the only thing they had to buy was furniture and the bits of crockery and cooking things.

Glenda thought she was in seventh heaven. A house to move into, a handsome husband, and he had a job. Little did she realise the Jekyll and Hyde character that lay beneath the charm. Oh, her Harry had a lovely smile. Of course he had, he was getting all he had planned.

She'll learn to do things my way soon enough. Run it like the army, that's the answer.

They went round to see Monica to invite her to the registry office wedding. Glenda wondered why Monica looked at her as if she was mad.

'Blimey,' she'd said, 'you must be daft taking him on. I wouldn't take any man on, that's for sure.'

Must have been let down by someone, and it's soured her, thought Glenda.

They got married on a Thursday morning, this being the best day for Monica, had a meal in a public house and then parted, Monica to her own home.

'Good luck,' she'd said to Glenda. 'You'll need it.'

Glenda got herself a job cleaning, which didn't interfere with looking after Harry. They had furniture on hire purchase, which had to be paid for, and Glenda soon learned she would have to pay for it. Harry gave her housekeeping money and it was enough if she was careful, and she learned to be very careful indeed. She also learned very quickly that the man who had courted her and the man she had married were two different people. Very demanding and very rough in his lovemaking, and Glenda felt every time she'd been through a wringer. She soon found, however, that it was better to say nothing, or Harry would get even more violent.

My God, what have I let myself in for? she'd asked herself.

She really knew when she'd told him she was pregnant. It took her days to get over the shock of his attack on her. It was then that she knew she was trapped like a bird in a cage, and Harry knew that she knew it and played on it. This indeed did satisfy the bloodlust within him, for he had his punchbag all neat and tidy at home whenever he needed it. Lovely, it was.

Chapter Twelve

1956–1957

Glenda sat at the kitchen table with her head in her hands. She felt as if she had been in a fight with a steamroller. She hurt all over and one look at her face in the bathroom mirror that morning had shown her that this was another day when she would not be able to leave the house. Her cheeks were swollen and already showing the bruising that would come out in a couple of days. Her eyes were sore and one nearly closed with the swelling. Where he had punched her body last night was so painful she didn't know how she was to get on with the housework, but she must, or she would get more of the same tonight. And it all started because I'd got meat pie for dinner instead of a roast, she thought. I shall never please him, but I'm stuck here. I can't go because I have nowhere to go where I can take the children. She felt the tears stinging her cheeks.

She had two children – Mark, aged eight years, and six-year-old Samantha. They had looked at her this morning and had not said a word, they knew better than that. One word and they knew their mother would get more abuse. They didn't know what went on in the bedroom of course.

Glenda thought back to the time when she had first told Harry she was pregnant with Mark. So foolish I was, she thought. I thought he would be so pleased to be a father. But life is strange, for instead, Glenda found a different man before her. She thought he had suddenly gone mad with joy, for he had charged around the room, then, without warning, he had come straight towards her. Instead of taking her in his arms he had knocked her to the floor. The shock was so great she just lay there.

'Get up, get up,' Harry had yelled. 'If you think I'll treat you like an invalid you're mistaken. What do you think you are doing getting pregnant? When did I ever say I wanted children?'

He kicked her in the back and yelled again. 'Get up, slut, and get my meal.'

Glenda pulled herself up from the floor, tears streaming down her face, and lurched over to the cooker.

'I thought you'd be pleased,' she sobbed.

'Pleased!' he'd shrieked. 'What do we want with kids? They're nothing but a damned nuisance, and, slut, if you think I'm going to help you with it, think again, you're on your own.'

The scene went through Glenda's mind, and then all the months when the baby was growing, teething problems, measles, and crying in the night.

Things had gone from bad to worse. The more the baby needed her, the more Harry had shown his temper.

Then she found she was pregnant again, only this time it was worse. Baby Mark was in his cot upstairs which was just as well, for she was knocked from one side of the room to the other. Even though she was in pain and pregnant, he wanted her body every night. She knew without doubt then that she had married a sadistic man, but she had no living relatives and couldn't make friends because Harry disapproved, and anyway, her face was bruised so much she only went out when she had to.

What was the good of telling the doctor or the clinic? She had no money of her own and no place to go.

Sometimes she thought it would be better to end it all and take the children with her, but she couldn't take their lives.

Whenever she bought clothes or gifts for them she suffered for it, but she put up with it for the children's sake. Christmas was the worst time, and their birthdays. She knew they were afraid of their father, and she knew that if he laid one finger on them she would kill him and gladly swing for it.

Monica, Harry's sister, came round and did try to help. Although Glenda wasn't all that keen on her, she had to accept help where she could get it.

'Harry always did have a temper, even as a little boy,' Monica said. 'Of course, he was spoilt rotten by Mum, and never could do anything wrong. I always got the blame for anything that happened just because I was older than him. I was surprised that he took so long to show his real colours.'

Monica came about once a week, lighting one cigarette after another and puffing smoke all over the house. Glenda always opened the windows wide to let out the fog – after she left, that was, of course; if Harry wasn't home, she wouldn't dare if he was there.

Monica was coming today, and Glenda knew she would have to get up and make some effort to tidy up the rooms. First some painkillers, she thought, and went up to the bathroom. She was lucky with Mark and Samantha. They always left everything tidy and she knew they did this to help her. Mark had said once, 'When I grow up, Mummy, I'm going to take you away from here, and if Daddy tries to get you back I'll knock him black and blue, just you see.'

'Sweetheart,' she'd said, 'don't ever get so violent over anything, it's not worth it. You do yourself more harm in the end, because once you start that, you won't be able to stop it.'

She spent the morning cleaning as best she could, then got herself some soup. It's amazing what the body can take, she thought. I go about my work as if nothing was wrong; it must be that I've got so used to being a punchbag that I don't care anymore. I'll go on trying to get this place looking decent even if it does mean more bruises on old bruises. I must do it for the children's sake. We can't live in a slum.

Fortunately, Harry didn't keep her short of money, but he did want her to account for every penny, which she did to keep the peace, for the sake of Mark and Samantha.

Two o'clock came, and Monica appeared, smoking the inevitable cigarette.

'Oh, I can see he's been at it again,' she said. 'I don't know how you put up with it.'

'You put up with anything when you've got children,' Glenda replied.

'Well, you'd better tell me if you want some shopping and I'll get it for you before I settle myself,' Monica said. 'You won't be going anywhere for a day or two, I can see that.'

Glenda handed her the list she had made and some money, and Monica left in her usual haze of smoke.

Shutting the front door, Glenda thought, I wish I could like her more than I do. She does try to help, and I should be thankful. Oh, I am, but I wish things were normal here.

She turned back to the kitchen to get the tea and cakes ready for Monica's return. Halfway down the passage, she stopped. Hell, she thought. Why should I keep hiding away? From tomorrow I'll make myself go out, if I only walk round the park. At least it will be a change from four walls. I'll go nutty if I keep living my life like this.

The next day was sunny though chilly. Early spring, she thought. Well, at least I can wrap a scarf round my neck and most of my face, and sunglasses hide bruises, don't they?

Shutting the front door behind her, she felt a great sense of release, like getting out of prison. Just a little walk, she thought. Start thinking about my life. I can't go on like this or I'll end up dead, and God help my children then.

She made her way to the park, and walked along by the lake. There she sat on a bench. She didn't notice the wind, so wrapped up in her thoughts was she. Vaguely, she felt someone sit on the bench with her, and jumped when a man's voice said, 'Would it help to talk about it?'

Only then did she realise she was crying.

'I come here most days,' said the same voice. 'I used to bring my old dog here. Just had to have him put down. It's a place the wife and I used to come to, but she died a couple of years back with cancer, but I still come here. It gives me a kind of peace, really.'

What a funny way to cry, thought Glenda. I'm not making any noise, but the tears are falling. I must be in a bad way.

She felt something put into her lap, and when she looked through the haze of tears, it was a handkerchief. She wiped her cheeks and handed it back to the man beside her.

'Thank you, but I have to go now, I've got two children to see to, and they'll be home from school soon.' She stood up and looked at him and saw a thin man with a heavy coat and a scarf round his neck. His face was full of concern, and she noticed his brown eyes with heavy eyebrows.

'I come here most days,' he said, 'just for a while. It's better than sitting alone all the time. I'll look for you whenever I come, and perhaps we can talk your grief out of you.'

'Thank you, but I don't know when I'll be able to get away again. It's always a bit difficult.'

'No matter, I'll be here whenever you do come. I'll see you sometime, I'm sure.'

Glenda turned away to go home. I'd better get dinner straight on, she thought, or there'll be more trouble. Still, somehow she felt lighter and more able to cope.

The children came home full of their stories about school, but they were not exuberant as children should be. They're living on a knife edge just like me, she thought. Whatever am I going to do? It's wrong for them, they ought to be running around shouting and happy, but they're afraid, like me, of putting a foot wrong. What a life for them, poor little devils.

She made their meal for them and they went upstairs to their rooms as usual, for they were not allowed to be downstairs when Harry came home. Everything had to be quiet and peaceful, not a sound anywhere.

As she put the final touches to the meal for them both, she heard his key in the door. The usual tension started rising within her. She prayed there would not be any trouble tonight.

He came in, looked around and went straight upstairs to change. No word of greeting, nothing, but that was quite usual. The only time he spoke it was to belittle her over some stupid thing. She had learned long ago to keep quiet.

He came into the dining room as she was putting the last dish onto the table. Silently he served himself, and silently she too served herself.

This is like being in Victorian times, she thought. The master ruling the roost.

She cleared the first course away and served the sweet. Still the silence. He's working himself up, as always, for a few days, then all hell will be let loose again. Glenda sat forcing down the food. No matter how she felt she had to eat or he'd be in one of his rages, and the outcome of those she tried to avoid at all costs.

When they had finished, he went into the lounge where he waited every night for her to wash up and clear away before she brought in the coffee. The routine was always the same.

After she had cleared the coffee things and washed them and put them away, he would inspect everywhere to make sure it was to his liking.

Tonight, while she worked, she thought of the man in the park. His voice, full of peace and compassion, came back to her. He obviously thinks I've just lost my husband. If only he knew what a blessing that would be. Shocked at herself, she stared into space. Somehow I'll get myself and the children out of this, she thought. One day he is going to go too far and kill me. But how? Where do I go? How will I keep us? The only way is to look for a housekeeper's job, but how will I go for an interview, I can't get away. Dear God, help us, help me.

She turned towards the lounge, where the television was blaring out. Time to get the children to bed, then she had to endure the evening sitting with him. Endure is the right word, she thought. I hate him so much I could kill him. I will too, if he lays one hand on Mark or Samantha. The little boy and girl had washed and got themselves undressed, ready for bed. They're old before their years. They shouldn't be doing this alone, she thought.

'Goodnight, Mummy.' And giving her a big kiss and a gentle hug, they went into their bedrooms. She tucked them in and kissed them goodnight. Mark said, 'One day we'll all be happy, Mummy, you'll see.'

As she left them, she thought to herself, Yes, one day, but when?

Chapter Thirteen

The days went by, with the same routine following day after day. The weekend came and went, with Mark and Samantha playing quietly in the garden with each other, and being ready for bed by the time their father was in. Whatever happened, they never left their room because he had told them they mustn't.

Once a week, she went to the park and the same kind man was always there. On the days when she had to cover bruises she wore long sleeves and sunglasses and a scarf high round her face.

One day he said to her, 'Why do you always cover yourself up so much? I've no idea what you look like really.' So that day she took off her glasses and the scarf and watched the horror come into his face. 'My God, how did you get like this?' Then the truth dawned on him. 'You're nearly always like that, aren't you? What happens?'

Glenda found herself telling him of her life, of the children and Harry. She was amazed at herself for being so matter of fact about it all.

'What I need is a job where I can take the children, far away where he can never find us,' she said finally.

'What you need,' he replied, 'is a visit to a doctor, a lawyer and a marriage guidance counsellor.'

'No, that's no good. They would all want to see Harry and it would only make things worse. It doesn't matter about me, but if he touches my children I'll kill him stone dead.'

'Well let me think about it all. My name, by the way, is Charles, but everyone has always called me Charlie. There must be some answer somewhere and I'll find it. Just give me time. You haven't told me your name, and we've been meeting here for the past four weeks.'

'Glenda,' she said. 'I'll come back when I can, and believe me I'll try to find a way out too. I only keep going for my children, life has no meaning but for them.'

'He's a monster, he should be put away. Somehow there must be a way to get you all away before murder is done by one or other of you.'

As they parted, Glenda wrapped her scarf round her head again and put on her glasses. It had started to rain so she hurried to get home. At least she didn't feel quite so alone now, but could still see no answer to her problems.

Life went on as usual, with Harry having his periodic outbursts over little things. It might be that she made a noise putting out the dishes for dinner or that the meal was not what he wanted, not that she ever knew what he wanted each day, for he never said. Everything was just an excuse to use his fists on her. She knew time was running out because the attacks were becoming more frequent and more severe. She now had scars where the skin broke open when his fist hit it, but that was always at night on her body. She'd learned never to cry out, for that made him worse, and anyway she couldn't bear to hear the sound of the children crying themselves to sleep. She knew she would have to get away, even if she walked the streets for a few nights until she found a place for the three of them.

It was now about eight or nine months since she had first met Charlie, the only bright thing in her life, except the children of course. He always talked quietly, never raising his voice, and his sense of humour bordered on the ridiculous.

Mostly he talked about his wife, and often brought in some amusing detail about his dog. She understood how lonely he felt, and his aloneness, but his aloneness was different from hers.

She felt how lucky his wife must have been to have a husband like Charlie. He'd nursed her at home until she died in his arms early one morning. 'I shall always love her,' he'd said. 'We couldn't have children but that didn't matter, though we both would have liked them. Still, God didn't see fit to give them to us so we had to put up with it. We had started talking about fostering or adopting, but didn't think we would stand much chance of adopting because of our ages, both being in our late thirties. Still, we thought we might be considered for foster parents.' He sat looking out across the lake, and Glenda didn't disturb him, knowing he was back with his wife in his thoughts.

Why couldn't Harry have been like Charlie? she thought. How much happier and better life would be for us all. Mark and Samantha should be laughing and running around instead of being afraid to move. No, life can't go on like this, I've got to get away somehow, for their sakes.

Charlie shifted in his seat. 'Well anyway, when she discovered the lump it was too late. She was operated on but the cancer had spread too far. In less than a year she was dead. I thought at first I'd go mad, but the old dog helped me, but now of course he's gone, poor old boy. You can't keep them when they're suffering, it's not right.' He looked at her wearing her dark glasses. 'How much longer are you going to put up with the beatings your husband gives you? Isn't it time you did something?'

'Such as what?' she said. 'Where do I go? I've got children, you know, and if I roam the streets with them they'll be taken away from me and could be given to my husband to care for. It wouldn't be long before he started on them in his tempers. He hasn't done so yet, and if he lays one finger on either of them I shall take up the nearest knife and kill him. He's got to sleep sometime. I think he knows this, and so far hasn't pushed me beyond that limit.'

'Well anyway,' Charlie said to her, 'you keep coming here when you can and we'll see what can be worked out. I'll put my mind to it. I've got friends who will know what's to be done. Try to keep going until I can get something worked out.'

'Charlie, you're the bright spot in my life, and my lifeline,' Glenda said. 'Your wife was a very lucky woman to have you.'

'No, I think *I* was the lucky one to have her. You would have liked her. She wasn't beautiful in the usual sense of the word, but there was an inner beauty about her that you could sense. I know she'd want me to help you, she was that kind of lady.' Charlie stood up to go. 'Remember, I'll be here every day I can, and we'll work something out.' He turned to leave.

Glenda watched him go, then got up to leave this place of peace in her life. Back to the torture, she thought.

The next time she went to the park, Charlie was there as usual.

'I thought you wouldn't be coming today,' he said. 'I seem to have waited ages, but that's because I've got things to tell you. I've been very busy since I saw you last.'

'Charlie, I don't want you to get into any trouble over me.' Glenda sat there, looking across the lake. 'I don't think you fully realise what kind of man my husband is. He's violent, yes, but he works out in his mind for days before the violent times what he will pick on and what he will do. I have a horrible feeling you will get in too deep and get hurt. I'd never forgive myself if anything happened to you.'

Glenda realised for the first time how much Charlie had come to mean to her. Life without him around somewhere really had no meaning. Her children meant the world to her, but Charlie was different. She felt his goodness and felt afraid for him, but didn't know why.

'I don't see that anything can happen to me,' Charlie said. 'What I have in mind at this point in time is just for you and your children. None of you can go on the way you are. Putting you to one side, think of your children. Their lives are not how they should be. What kind of adults will they be growing up into, the way they are? Do you want them to be so mixed up in their minds they will never be able to live their adult lives properly? Think of them first and foremost.'

'I do,' she replied. 'That's all I ever think of, but I still end up in the same circle and back to the beginning again.'

'Well then, listen to what I have to say, and when I have finished, say nothing. Just go home and think about my proposals and I'll see you next week and you can tell me your answer.'

The wind was cold and the sky overcast. With no one else around, it seemed to Glenda that they were in a world of their own.

'When my wife Laura became ill, I gave up my business, sold out. I have no money worries at all. We had a small cottage where we used to go for weekends or holidays up near Wales in the Forest of Dean.' Charlie looked at her. 'What I suggest is that, when the children start their Christmas holiday, you tell them you will all go out for the day. Get yourselves to Victoria coach station and I will arrange a car to pick you up and take you to the cottage. You mustn't say anything to them beforehand, and bring no luggage. However good they are, if you tell them, they might let something slip before the day. I have arranged with a doctor friend in Oxford that you will be examined and X-rayed, and a report written out by him to be sent to my solicitor.'

'Charlie, how can I do this?' Glenda cried. 'You don't realise the danger to you. If Harry found out about you, he would kill you. You don't know him as I do. His brain is so twisted it's like a corkscrew.'

'I told you say nothing until I had finished, then you can think about it and start planning. Now, when you've seen the doctor, whose name I shall not tell you until we are at the hospital, we will then proceed to the cottage. It's in a remote part of the Forest of Dean, and it's unlikely that your husband will find you. In any case, all correspondence will then be through my solicitor. My name will not be mentioned, not even as your landlord. I've spoken to my solicitor, whose name again you won't know until the right time. He thinks your children can be made wards of the court, so your husband can never have access to them except through a court hearing. When you have had time to settle into the cottage, you can write down all the facts for my solicitor about your life with your husband, the way the children have been treated and yourself. I think a divorce court will take a dim view of it all. You will not need to ask for any money from your husband to keep you or your children. I have sufficient money to take care of all your needs.'

'Oh, Charlie, how can I let you do all this? The children are Harry's and he should at least keep them, even if he never wanted them near him.'

'Now what did I say? Already you raise obstacles before the act is done. What a woman! Don't you know that I love you, and if your children are like you then I'm sure we shall get on fine. I, of course, shall not be with you until after the divorce, because we don't want complications. I'm just the landlord. We have to have you and the children protected from your husband at all costs. Let's see, the holidays start in about two weeks, don't they? That will give me time to stock up the cottage in case you are snowed in for weeks. There's a nice neighbour who keeps an eye on the place and looks after the letting for me, because I haven't used it since my wife went, couldn't face it, but if I feel I can help you, and most of all, your children, I will feel that Laura has not died in vain. All I know is that she keeps telling me to help your children. Sounds silly, doesn't it?'

'No, Charlie, it doesn't sound silly. I think your Laura must have been a wonderful person. I only wish I had known her. Harry's got a sister, Monica. She tries to help. Visits once a week and shops for me if I can't go out. She's good, but I still can't like her very much. I feel sorry for her really. She apparently always got the beatings that Harry deserved when they were children because, being older than him, her mother thought she should always take care of him. She's never surprised when she comes and finds me with black eyes. I think she takes it all as a matter of course. She never married, though I think there have been plenty of men friends in her life. Still, I suppose she thought that no way was she going to put up with my life, she'd had enough beatings as a child. I don't think she cares for her brother much. She's good to the children as far as she can be, but again, Harry gets bouts of temper whenever she brings something, even for Christmas, so now she just gives me money and I buy clothes for them.'

'However good your husband's sister might be, you must not say anything to her. Keep everything to yourself, or something may slip out. When I see you next week you can give me your answer, and if you agree to my proposals I'll set everything in motion for whatever day you say. You've got to do something, Glenda, love, and the longer you wait, it seems to me the more danger there is for you all. I'm leaving now and I'll see you here next week sometime. God bless, my dear.' As he turned to go Glenda realised that never once had he so much as touched her. She sat for a while, her mind in a turmoil. Could it be that at last an answer had come to her prayers? Oh, dear God, she hoped so. She got up and turned for home. She must make sure all was well tonight so that she could think, while Harry watched the interminable television.

If she sat knitting, he would think she was concentrating on that. She'd have to be careful though, and make sure she heard him if he spoke to her, which would only be an order for something to eat or drink, never conversation. She looked at her watch and realised that she must hurry to get home before the children. No matter what happened, everything must be the same.

Chapter Fourteen

During the following week, each day was a replica of the one before. She knew that Harry was working something out to spoil the Christmas holiday for Mark and Samantha, because always there had to be something to spark off one of his rages just as the holidays were starting. Each day, she watched the children become quieter, and knew that they too were waiting for the outburst. She had already made her mind up about Charlie's offer. Enough is enough, she thought. If I don't kill Harry, Mark will. And that she couldn't let happen.

When she went to the usual bench in the park, Charlie was waiting.

'I'll take up your offer,' she said. 'I just can't go on the way I am.'

'When do Mark and Samantha start their Christmas holiday?'

'This weekend, on Friday, and they don't go back to school for three weeks, I think.'

Charlie smiled at her. 'Well, if all goes to plan, they won't be going to school there again. How old are they and when are their birthdates?'

Glenda told him and felt surprise that Mark would be nine at the end of January and Samantha seven years old in March. She thought how awful it was that they had to think in grown-up ways over so many things, and yet they were little more than babies.

'Right,' Charlie broke in on her thoughts, 'get the three of you to Victoria coach station on Monday next by 10 a.m., and I will be there to pick you up. The car will look more like a minicab, the colour green, and it's a Ford Cortina. No luggage, remember. As far as the neighbours and everyone are concerned, you will be taking your children out for the day. Will you have enough money to get you all to Victoria?'

'Oh yes, that's about the only good thing, he's never kept me short of money, but I do have to account for every penny.'

'Well, this is one accounting you won't be doing, but there again, it's one thing in his favour in the divorce proceedings.' Charlie grinned. 'I feel quite light-hearted, happier than I have been since Laura went. Silly, I know, because I won't be with you for some time, but I feel I've just been given the family we always wanted. I know they haven't met me yet, but I hope they won't fear me when they do.'

'They are quite used to behaving like church mice,' Glenda said, 'and it will take a while for them to come out of that. Still, I have no doubts when they get to know you they will love you like I do.'

'I hope so, because I love their mother very much. We've never so much as touched each other, yet I feel so close to you, it's wonderful.'

'That's the way I feel, Charlie, and we still can't touch each other. Our minds and hearts can be together, though.'

'Our day will come, Glenda, love, just you wait and see.'

Glenda felt a cold shiver go right through her. Dear God, she thought, don't let anything happen to Charlie.

'Look, the sky has come out blue for us,' Charlie said, grinning. 'A good omen, I would say. Whatever happens before Monday, get yourself to Victoria coach station, even if you have to have a taxi to do it. If you have a bank account of any kind, draw it all out and close the account. We don't want him to have any way of finding you. Have we thought of everything? I've got the cottage stocked with food for your arrival, and I've arranged with the neighbour to have the electricity and gas on, so everything should be ready for us when we get there. I'll pack a hamper with food so you don't have to think about that, and we'll cook when we get there. Anything else?'

'School, Charlie,' Glenda said. 'Where will the children go to school?'

'Oh, I've thought of that too. There's a retired schoolteacher in the village and she says she will tutor your children until the end of the summer term anyway. By that time they should have got to know some of the other children in the village and come out of their shells a bit, and going to school will be good for them by then. I shall, of course, come home here and sell my house, then when that's settled we can be together. I'll see you at weekends when I can, though.'

Glenda felt she was in a dream-world and that she would wake up soon, back to the reality of her life.

'Take care of yourself until I see you on Monday, then you can start a new life. Take it as done that I have kissed you, and do be careful, we don't want anything to go wrong now, do we?'

They parted, each for their own home, and Glenda felt she was walking on air, but as she neared her home, the ever-present fear returned. She knew something would happen this weekend because that was the routine before every school holiday.

Everything was peaceful through the rest of the week, but as the days passed, Glenda knew that the weekend would be the time. Saturday was quiet, and by the evening her nerves were at screaming pitch. Mark and Samantha played quietly in the garden and came in at four o'clock to have their meal before going upstairs. They were never noisy, never argued, and were always obedient. Just two more days, my babies, Glenda thought, then we'll be free, please God.

Harry went out as usual to his golf, and he would do the same tomorrow. The weekends never varied. By the time bedtime came she thought she would scream, and there was still tomorrow; and if nothing happened tonight, then it would be tomorrow. He plays with me like a cat with a mouse, she thought.

Sunday came and the day was as the Saturday. She was putting the final dishes on the dining table when Harry came in. His face was like a thundercloud. This is it, she thought, and before the thought had finished he was yelling at her.

'You stupid bitch, can't you think of any other meal than roast lamb, roast beef, or roast pork for a Sunday? What's in these dishes, eh? Roast potatoes, oh yes, we must have roast potatoes, mustn't we? Greens, oh we can't do without our greens, can we? You never did have any imagination. It doesn't occur to you I might not want roast every Sunday, does it, does it?' He pushed her away from the table so forcefully she nearly fell where she was. God help me, she was thinking as he turned towards the table.

'You can keep your potatoes,' he yelled, throwing the dish at her. It caught her just below her right eye. 'And your stupid greens, and the meat, slut, keep the lot and eat it off the floor, where you belong.' Another dish hit her in the chest, and the hot roast struck her straight in the face, the hot juices splattering over her. She put her arms up to defend herself, and as she did so, he punched her heavily in the ribs. As she toppled sideways, he kicked her in the back. 'Stupid cow, I married a stupid cow,' he shrieked at her. 'Get this cleaned up before I get back,' and as he passed her he kicked twice more in her back.

Glenda lay there, the hot meat juices and vegetables scalding her face. Her back and ribs felt like red-hot pokers.

'I'll be in at ten and want his place spick and span or you'll get another dose, mark me, woman, you will.' As she passed out, she heard his laughter, and then the door slam.

The next thing Glenda heard was Mark's voice.

'Mummy, Mummy, wake up.'

She opened her eyes and saw that he was crying. She tried to sit up but everything went round and round. Must make an effort, she thought. Can't have Mark downstairs when he comes back.

'Mark, go into the kitchen and bring a tea towel soaked in cold water,' she said, and wondered why her voice was slurred. The little boy got up and ran to do her bidding. When he came back, he found his mother had got herself off the floor and was sitting in a chair.

'There you are, Mummy,' he said. 'Your face is all swollen and red.'

She started wiping her face and found the towel was red with blood, and looking down at her dress she saw the blood and vegetables had smothered the front of it.

'Help me upstairs, darling,' she said to Mark. 'I must change my clothes. While I do that I want you and Samantha to get dressed. Put on all your warmest clothes, three of each thing. Be quick, both of you. Wrap yourselves up well in scarves, and put on your warmest coats and shoes. We are leaving here tonight.'

'Leaving?' Mark looked stunned. 'Where to, Mummy? Where will we go?'

'I don't know, love, but just anywhere, anywhere away from here.'

'Mummy, when will you talk properly again? You're talking all funny.'

'Never mind that, lovey, just do as Mummy asks, will you?'

Mark went off and Glenda struggled to remove the dress. In the end she cut it off herself. The waves of nausea and giddiness kept coming and going, but she knew she had to go tonight, or she might not live until tomorrow. Where she would go, she didn't know. Not toward the High Road, that was for sure, for he would be in the pub somewhere there. She would have to take the back roads until she and the children were well away. Charlie had given her his phone number in case she needed him urgently. She had memorised it, and then thrown the paper away.

Mark came back with Samantha ready dressed, both their faces very solemn.

'Darlings, help Mummy to dress, I can't move without a lot of pain. I'm sorry, my angels, you have to see me like this. It's something I never wanted to happen.'

Samantha started crying. 'Poor Mummy, your face is all big.' She sobbed.

After much effort, Glenda was dressed. Every bit of clothing burned her, but she knew it was now or never. She picked up her handbag, checked the money and took them downstairs. As she reached the front door, she checked.

The back way, she thought, he never comes in the back way.

'Come on, we'll go out this way,' she said, leading them to the back door. 'Keep as quiet as you can and don't say a word until I speak to you. We don't want the neighbours to hear us.'

They crept silently down the garden path, out through the gate, and along the alleyway to the road. They turned away from the High Road, going along all the back turnings, until eventually they came to a telephone box. Taking note of the road name and the name of a church on the corner, she took them into the telephone booth.

'Dial this number for me, Mark.' She repeated the number bit by bit as he dialled. Her hands were shaking so much she could hardly hold the hand piece. She had to lean back against the side of the box to keep herself upright. The ringing tone seemed to go on for ages, then the receiver was lifted and she heard Charlie's voice. 'Charlie, Charlie,' was all she could manage to say before she was choking on tears. She passed the receiver to Mark. When he put it to his ear, he heard a man's voice saying, 'Glenda, what's wrong, answer me, love.'

'Mr Man,' said Mark, 'my mummy needs you. We are in a telephone box, and there is a church over the road called St Anthony's. We've walked from home, and Mummy is very hurt. Please come, Mr Man.'

'Is that Mark?' said the man.

'Yes, I'm Mark. Mummy looks as if she is going to faint. Please come.'

'Mark, ask Mummy what the name of the road is where you are.'

'Yes,' said Mark. 'Mummy, what's the name of this road?'

Glenda pulled herself together and took the receiver from Mark. 'It's Rendall Road, Charlie, and St Anthony's is over the road. It's the other side of town from the park. Please come, I need you.'

'Stay where you are, all of you. I'll be there soon. Keep in the box in the warm. If anyone comes to use the phone, pretend you're making a call, but don't move. Sweetheart, be strong now. I'll be with you soon.'

The phone went down with a bang.

'We've to stay here until he comes,' said Glenda. 'You'll like him, he's a very kind man.'

'When did you meet him, Mummy?' said Samantha.

Glenda drew her daughter to her. 'Oh, not so long ago. He had a wife, but she went to Heaven to be with Jesus, and then he had to send his dog too. We met in the park and he's been my friend ever since.'

'He won't be like Dad and hit you, will he?' said Mark.

'No, lovey, he won't.' Glenda found she had slipped further and further down the side of the telephone booth until she was on the floor. Every bit of her hurt. She felt as if she had hot pokers all over her. She drifted off into stupor, coming to again when she heard Mark say, 'There's a car going slowly along the road towards us, Mummy. Is it him?'

Glenda turned her head toward the road and saw that the car had stopped outside the church. She saw Charlie get out and look over toward the telephone box. 'Go out to him, Mark, go out to him before he goes away,' she said.

Mark opened the door as the man crossed the road toward him.

'Hello,' he said. 'Are you Mark?'

'Yes I am, and Mummy is on the floor in the box. She seems to be going to sleep. I expect she is very tired,' said Mark.

'Let's see what we can do then,' said Charlie. 'We'll have to get her where she can sleep, won't we?'

He opened the door of the telephone box and looked at Glenda. 'My God,' he said. 'You'd better stay there until I bring the car over, you'll never walk it.'

When he'd got the car close to where they were, he lifted Glenda up and put her on the front seat. 'In the back with you both,' he said to Mark and Samantha. 'Let's get home and see to your mummy, the sooner the better.'

Chapter Fifteen

Charlie drove round to the back of his house. He dashed in and brought out blankets and pillows, then put the kettle on to make soup for the children.

While the kettle boiled, he telephoned his friend Dr Makinson, who had the private hospital in Oxford.

'Roger, it's Charlie,' he said when the telephone was answered. 'You remember the lady I told you about with the violent husband? Yes? Good. Well, I've got her and the children in my car right now. He's given her a real beating this time. If I bring her straight to your clinic, could you see her tonight? She's not fit to be moved again, and I don't want to get a doctor round here, for obvious reasons.' He listened for a while. 'Yes, she's bad. I think it's more the trauma of the attack, although she *is* injured. I could get to you in an hour or so, is that all right? You'll be at the clinic waiting? Thanks, pal, you're great. I'll see you there.'

He went out to the car where Glenda was sitting staring before her. The children were sitting cuddled together in the back seat.

'Listen, little ones. I'm going in to pack a bag, make some soup and sandwiches for you, shut everything up, then we'll be off to take your mummy to a doctor friend of mine. Will you stay there and don't disturb Mummy? Wrap yourselves in the blankets. I won't be long.'

Within fifteen minutes he was back. 'Right, first some soup to warm you all up,' he said, 'and there's a sandwich if you want it. Snuggle in those blankets and keep warm, and I'll wrap Mummy up so she won't be cold, then we're off.'

With everyone settled, Charlie drove away. He saw with satisfaction that the children had gone to sleep. They must trust me, he thought, especially Mark. He would never have shut his eyes if he'd doubted me.

The car ate up the miles as Charlie drove steadily to Oxford, braking gently to avoid any further pain to Glenda.

It was about an hour and fifteen minutes later that they turned into the driveway of the private clinic, and pulled up outside the front door.

Mark woke up. 'Where are we?' he said. 'Where are you going?'

'I'm just going in there to tell my doctor friend we've arrived,' said Charlie. 'I won't be long, then we can get Mummy seen to. You look after her 'til I get back.'

Roger was waiting for him. 'I thought you'd never come,' he said.

'You'll need a wheelchair for her,' Charlie told him. 'And we need a place for the children for the night. They can't stay in the car all the time.'

'Well, let's get them in, shall we?' said Roger, and, signalling to a porter and a nurse, they went outside,

Glenda looked at them dazedly. She had no idea where she was except that she was safe. As they lifted her out she cried out in pain. Getting her undressed to be examined was a nightmare for her. Her clothes had stuck to the scalds on her chest and on the clotted blood from the broken areas where he had kicked her. She vomited and felt the room going round.

Roger said, 'You sure have taken a belting. How did the scalds happen? Looks like food was thrown at you, am I right?'

'Yes,' Glenda mumbled. 'The roast meat and veg, all of it.' Her speech was even more slurred and she found it very difficult to move her mouth. Oh, if only I could lie down and never move again, she thought.

She had to suffer the pain and indignity of a total examination followed by X-rays all over her body, head to toes. Finally her wounds were properly dressed and she was left to sleep for the rest of the night in a bed. She didn't worry about the children, because she knew Charlie would take care of them, and knew they would behave themselves. The last thing she remembered before drifting off to sleep was their little faces looking at her, then, as they kissed her, she fell into a dreamless sleep.

Roger arranged with his wife that Charlie and the children should stay with them overnight. Charlie was insistent that they all go on to Wales the next day, but what he wanted was a full and detailed report on the injuries present, and any old scars, internal or external that might show. Roger understood this, saying he wondered how she had put up with it so long if tonight was anything to go by.

When they arrived at Roger's home, the two children could not keep their eyes open. Charlie and Roger carried them up to the beds prepared for them, where Roger's wife undressed them and tucked them in, kissing each goodnight. She left a small light on in the room, in case they awoke and were frightened.

'No child should have to suffer the trauma those two have had,' she said as she came into the lounge. 'It's a barbaric situation. They're too frightened to open their mouths except to ask if their mummy is all right. If I got my hands on him, I'd give him such a going over.'

Roger laughed. 'He wouldn't know what had hit him,' he said. 'You with your judo holds, you'd tie him up in knots and have him screaming for mercy.'

'I would too, but I'd also give him a good taste of his own medicine, and how.' June's face was angry with her indignation. 'Face up to a bully and they back down,' she said.

'Well, I don't think he is a bully,' Charlie said. 'He seems to be a sadist to me. She never seems to have hit back from what I've heard, but I gather that was to protect her children.'

'Well, they'll do anything and put up with anything, I've always found, where they have children,' Roger agreed. 'It's not confined to one social class you know, it happens right through the scale, rich to poor, I know, I've seen them all. Anyway we should be thinking of bed for us all, busy day tomorrow.'

Mark awoke about eight the next morning. Seeing Samantha still asleep, he kept still. He thought over the things that had happened the previous night. Mummy's face looked like a big football, he thought. I wonder if it will ever go back like it was.

He didn't know what his father had done to Mummy, but knew it must be bad. He had never before seen her like that, so last night must have been worse than ever before. He hated his father with a terrible hate and only longed for the day when he was old enough to treat him as he had treated Mummy.

Samantha began to wake up. She started crying before she was fully awake. 'Mummy, I want Mummy.'

Mark turned over and put his arm over her. 'We'll see Mummy soon, Sam,' he said, but as he said it he found he was crying too.

Soon after, the door to their room opened and the man Mummy called Charlie came in, followed by the lady who had put them to bed.

'Wake up, little ones,' the man said. 'It's breakfast time.'

They both sat up in bed and Mark said, 'When will we see our mummy?'

'Well, when you've had your breakfast and Aunty June has got you both dressed we'll be away to the hospital. Can't go too early though, because your mummy won't be ready yet to see us. Uncle Roger has been in to see her already. You remember Uncle Roger, he's the nice doctor who saw your mummy last night. Here's Aunty June with your breakfast, nice scrambled egg on toast, you like that, don't you?' Charlie moved towards the bed, followed by June with a tray.

'Come on, babes, up you get and when you have had your breakfast, we'll see about getting you dressed, shall we?' June kissed them both on the top of the head and put up the pillows. 'Did you sleep well? I hope so, you were both dead tired last night. You were almost asleep before I'd got you undressed. Uncle Charlie will stay with you while you eat, then I'll be back, and then you can wash and dress, but you must have breakfast first. Can't start the day on nothing.'

Mark and Samantha sat up. Samantha had tears still streaming down her cheeks and her breath was catching with sobs.

'You poor little love,' June said. 'Let's sit you on my lap while you eat, sweetheart, come on.' She lifted her out of the bed and sat her on her lap by the bedside on a chair. 'Come on, Mark, let's see how much you can both eat, eh?'

'Eat up, Mark, we've a long journey ahead of us today, and we must be strong to look after your mummy. I'm sure she'll feel better today after a night's sleep.' Charlie smiled at Mark. 'You and I have to look after the ladies in the family, don't we?'

'I'll feel better and so will Sam when we see Mum. We've never been away from her before.' He looked at Charlie, alarmed. 'We're not going back home, are we?'

'No, lad, you are not, no way. We are going to a place where you can all rest and enjoy your Christmas. There will probably be lots of snow by then, and you can both play snowballs, and we'll make a big, big snowman, how about that?'

June said, laughing, 'You're nothing but a big kid yourself, Charlie. Bet you can't wait for the snow.'

Sam said, 'We've never made a snowman. How do you do that?'

'Ah well, just you wait. We'll make the biggest one we can,' Charlie said. 'Mark and you and me all together, that's if there is snow before Christmas, but I expect there will be where we are going.'

Some two hours later they were ready to leave for the clinic. June hugged both of them and said, 'I'll see you, young Mark, and you, Samantha, soon. It won't be until after Christmas because Uncle Roger has to work, but as soon after as we can make it.'

As they drove off, Samantha said, 'I like that lady, she's nice.'

They arrived at the clinic and went in. Charlie asked for Dr Makinson and they sat in the hallway to wait for him. When he came, he smiled at the children.

'I expect you'd like to see your mummy, wouldn't you? Won't be long now.'

A nurse came down the corridor towards them. 'She's ready now, Doctor, shall I take the children?' Roger nodded and she took the hand of each child and led them away.

'How is she, Roger? Is it all right for her to travel to my cottage today? The further away we get from her husband, the happier I shall be.'

'She'll travel, but will be unwell for many days yet. You'll have to get the local doctor and nurse in to her as soon as you get there. If you know the doctor's name and number, I'll ring him to tell him you're on your way. She really took a beating, you know. There are a lot of old bruises and scars. I shall write a full report of my findings for the solicitor. She's got fractured ribs but we can't strap her up because of the scalds, so we have bandaged her securely just for the journey. Don't want them to stay on for long though, because it does restrict the breathing, then she could be in worse trouble. We've dressed all the scalds we could and I've done the best I could to her face, but she will be scarred for life, that was quite a cut, and a cracked jawbone to boot. She's had a pasting many, many times. There are old rib fractures showing on the X-rays. I just hope he hasn't damaged her internal organs. How she walked I'll never know.'

Charlie looked at him. 'So she got away just in time then. The next lot would probably have been fatal?'

'Oh yes, I reckon so. Rape too, and not just once. The man must be a maniac. Anyway, I'll get my report done for you, don't worry.'

'My God,' Charlie was horrified. 'I doubt she'll ever get over it. My God.' He turned away, feeling sick in his body and sick at heart. The thought of any man behaving like that was beyond his reasoning powers.

Roger nudged him. 'Come on, old boy, you can't give way, she'll need you. Take it one day at a time, that's the only way she'll come round to clear thinking. Let's go and get her, shall we? Oh, and don't forget the doctor's number that I want.'

'No, I'll give it to you now, hang on.' Charlie looked round for a piece of paper and, finding a newspaper, tore a bit off. 'Got a pen?'

Roger handed him his, then put both pen and paper in his pocket when Charlie had finished writing. 'Let's go,' he said.

When they got to the ward door, Charlie forced a smile to his face and pushed it open. Glenda was sitting in a wheelchair ready for him. Her face was swollen and partly covered by bandages holding a dressing in place.

'Charlie.' She slurred the words, but her eyes, although swollen, shone. 'Take us with you,' she said slowly. 'Take us home with you.'

'That's where we are going right now. The car is all ready with blankets and pillows for you. We just have to get into it, love.'

'Doctor, thank you, and you, nurse. You have been kind.' The slurred slow words were whispered.

'Well, come on then,' Roger said. 'What are we hanging about for? Let's go.'

Glenda couldn't help crying out when they put her into the front of the car. Everywhere hurt.

'Let's strap you in and you can sleep all the way,' said Charlie. 'Hop in the back, children, and wrap those blankets round you. We're off on a new life.'

Chapter Sixteen

The long journey finally ended just as dusk was settling. They entered the drive of Charlie's cottage. Mrs Dowers, his neighbour, opened the door as soon as she heard the car pull into the drive.

'Hop out, children, and go into the house in the warm,' Charlie said. 'I've got to see about your mummy.'

As they got out and went into the house with Mrs Dowers, he turned to Glenda. 'I can't get you out on my own, love, so just stay still until I can get help.'

She turned her head. 'Charlie, you've been wonderful. I'll sit here until you come back, I couldn't move anyway.'

He found difficulty following what she said, for her face was so swollen now that the words all slurred into one, and she could only whisper, anyway. He put his hands on hers. 'We'll get you to bed, love, but I must get the doctor and nurse first.'

When he went in, he found Mrs Dowers had sat the children in the kitchen with her. She'd put hot milk and a hot meat pasty before them. She had removed their coats and hats, which were on a chair in the corner.

'Eat up, chuckies. Good bit of hot food will make you feel like ten people. I'll just see if I can help with your mum. Won't be long.'

She and Charlie went out into the hall. 'I must phone the doctor and nurse, Mrs Dowers, we can't get her out of the car on her own, she's bad. Will you get the bed ready upstairs for her so that she can go straight into it, please.'

'Well, after your call I put a single bed in the room in the front where the double is. I think if she's that bad she ought to go into the single one on her own, and the children can go into the double bed. Is that all right?'

'That's fine, my dear, you're an angel helping out like this. Now the phone, let's get things moving.'

An hour later, Dr Evans and Nurse Libby, as everyone called her, had got Glenda settled in her bed. Her wounds had been re-dressed, and the tight bandage round her chest loosened.

Glenda had passed out before they had finally got her out of the car, so ill and full of pain was she.

'I'll get you some painkillers for her, and Nurse will come in every day until she's recovered somewhat. Whatever happened to her, it was bad. I should think she'll withdraw into herself for a while, sort of defence mechanism. You are not going back home yet, are you?'

'Well, I did intend to originally, but this cropped up last night, and I don't see how I can leave her alone here with two young children. I'll certainly be here until the New Year, anyway.'

'Good, she'll need you, so will the children. I'm going to get Nurse Libby to talk to them in her official capacity, and so will I, then we'll get a report done, that's what you want, isn't it? She certainly can't go home to a monster like her husband. Dr Makinson told me what he had found, and he's sending a report to me, so we'll all be in the picture, won't we? Nurse will know when to call me. Just make sure she sleeps as much as she can for the next few days, that will let nature start the healing process. I'm not going to start her on tranquillisers because away from the stress she shouldn't need them. Anyway, I'm away for today, see you all tomorrow. You know my number, so call me if you need me.' Off he went and the nurse followed him a little later, saying she would come in the morning.

Charlie went down to Mrs Dowers and the children. As soon as he entered the kitchen, Mark ran to him.

'When can we see Mummy? Why have we had to wait so long?'

'Steady on, lad, you can see her now, come on, then we'll get her something she can suck through a straw, something nice and warm, but then she has to sleep. You are both sleeping in the big bed in her room, by the way.'

Mark looked up at Charlie, then flung his arms round his thighs. 'Thank you, Mr Man, for looking after us, we were ever so cold in the telephone box last night.'

Charlie hugged him close, and reached out his hand for little Samantha, who stood there wide-eyed.

'Go along you two, and see your mummy, then I'll come up with something nice for her.' Mrs Dowers pushed them all out of the room and turned back to the cooker. Somewhere there was a feeding cup Charlie's wife had used, if only she could remember where. Searching through the cupboards, she found it at last. She went to the larder and took the stew she'd made ready for next day. If she mashed all the vegetables and meat and put some gravy in the cup, perhaps that would do for the poor lady.

She carried the tray upstairs and found Mr Lambert and the children sitting on the edge of the double bed. Their mother seemed to be dozing but opened her eyes as soon as she went near the bed.

'I've brought you something to warm you up, my dear, then you can settle for the night and get some sleep. I'll see to the children, so don't you worry your head about nothing.'

'While you do that I'll see to the boiler and get the fuel in, ready for the morning. I'll see you when you've finished,' Charlie said, getting up off the bed. 'You two stay here with Mummy and Mrs Dowers, and I'll be back when I've finished.'

As Mrs Dowers started feeding Glenda, she heard the little girl say to her brother, 'Mark, I want to go to the toilet. I'll wet myself in a minute.' She put down the tray and told the children to follow her. She showed them the bathroom and asked if they had their night-clothes.

'We didn't bring anything,' said Mark. 'My mum didn't say anything about that.'

'Oh well, never you mind, I'll have to see what I can find, won't I, loveys,' she said. 'Come back to the bedroom when you've done and I'll tend to you when I've finished feeding your mummy.'

Glenda could manage very little and a lot of food spilled out of her mouth. She found opening her mouth very painful and felt so sick, but she tried to please this kind soul who seemed to have taken so much trouble over her. She was so tired all she wanted to do was sleep, but she knew that she had to try for the sake of Mark and Samantha. Finally the food was finished, though really she hadn't had much of it.

'Now, my dears, I'm going along to my daughter to borrow some clothes for you all. She's got quite a family of kids and won't mind. Tomorrow I'll have to go shopping. We won't be able to leave that to Mr Lambert. Men never know what to buy, do they?'

Glenda wanted to say that her husband wouldn't have bought the children anything if it had been left to him, but couldn't get the words out.

'Never you mind about trying to talk, my dear, you can do that when you are better. Now, babes, stay with Mummy 'til I come back. Won't be long.'

As she left the room, Mark and Samantha went over to their mother. 'Mummy, will we stay here?' Mark said. Glenda nodded her head and mouthed, 'Yes.'

'Good,' he said. 'We like it here, and that Mr Man is ever so kind. He's going to make a snowman, he said, but only when the snow comes. I hope it comes soon so we can start. We don't have to go back home, do we?'

Glenda shook her head, though it hurt her to do so.

'Can we sit on your bed, Mummy?'

It hurt her to shake her head at her daughter, who was, after all, little more than a baby.

''Course not, Sam, that will make Mummy hurt more, won't it?' Mark said. 'We are going to sleep in that big bed so we'll be near Mummy if she needs anything. We've both got to be good and help to make Mummy better, that's right, isn't it, Mum?'

Glenda put out her hand to them and they stood there holding it like two little leeches.

As the week passed, Glenda lay in her bed and felt as if she was suspended in time. The only reality was that she felt safe. All tension that she had felt for so many years seemed to have left her and sometimes she wondered if she had died, but then, if she had, so had her children because she saw them so often. She had no idea where she was and this did not worry her. She knew Charlie was around somewhere, because she saw him too.

She awoke from her sleep one day and heard children laughing. Must be near a school, she thought, then realised that she was hearing Charlie's voice, and little Mark was shouting. Whatever they were doing, they were enjoying it, she thought as she drifted back to sleep.

She woke up again as the bedroom door opened and the lady who kept coming in and out of the room every day came in with a tray in her hands.

'Come, lovey, let's see if we can eat this up, shall we? Your mouth is not so swollen today, so let's try, shall we?'

Glenda tried to sit up and, to her surprise, managed to do so without too much pain.

Before her was placed a tray with baked fish and bread and butter. She looked at the lady who had brought it in.

'I don't know your name,' she said, 'but I know you have been coming in to see me, and others too, but I don't know them either.' Her speech was clearer now and so was her mind, and she found herself thinking of Harry. 'Where am I, how did I get here? The last thing I remember is me and the children in a telephone box. Where's Charlie? Charlie came, I know.'

'Now, now, don't get all worked up. You are quite safe and so are your children, they're with Mr Lambert. My name is Mrs Dowers and I look after Mr Lambert when he's here, as I did when his poor dear wife was alive. You eat that up, lovey, have a little sleep afterwards and then you can talk all you want. I'll be back in a few minutes when I've served the others. Such games they've been having. We've had snow and he's been out there with the kiddies, like a big kid himself. I haven't seen him so happy since his wife was well.'

She left Glenda, forcing her to feed herself. Much to her amazement, she found she was hungry, and although she ate all on the plate, when Mrs Dowers came back she found Glenda sleeping again.

Good, she thought. That'll do her more good than anything.

When she got downstairs, she told the others that Glenda was sleeping and to leave her be. They could all go up when she woke up and have tea together. Charlie, Mark and Samantha looked at her, and then each other, and nodded, nudging each other as they did so.

'Cheeky lot,' Mrs Dowers said as she turned to do the washing up. Charlie got up from the table. 'Come on, maties, let's help clear the dishes and wash up. I think Mrs Dowers deserves to put her feet up and have a nice cup of tea, don't you?'

Mark and Samantha nearly fell off their seats in their haste to help. When everything was cleared away, Charlie made the tea.

'Get the stool, Mark, and you sit down, Mrs Dowers, it's *your* turn to be waited on now.'

Samantha carried the tea cup full of tea very carefully to Mrs Dowers. She leaned up to give her a kiss.

'That's because I love you,' she said. 'You've got to put your feet on the stool and sit there, hasn't she, Uncle Charlie?'

'Yes indeed she has, and we've got to be quiet like church mice. You never know, she might doze off, so let's sit here and make paper chains, then we can hang them up tonight. What do you say about that?'

Mark and Samantha sat themselves back at the table while Uncle Charlie brought out the gum and packets of paper.

'We want them as long as you can make them,' he said. 'We've got a lot of ceiling to cover in the front room. Oh, what a Christmas we'll have!'

'Can we hang our socks up?' asked Mark.

'You can hang a pillowcase up, little ones, and see if Father Christmas fills it. How about that?'

'Ooh, Uncle Charlie, will he really?' cried Samantha. 'He never has before, has he, Mark? Daddy always said he never would because we were such horrible children, but do you think if we are very good he'll leave us something?'

'Well, I've already sent a letter to him to tell him where you are, so I expect he's got some toys ready for you.'

'Why, they're dear little mites.' Mrs Dowers almost choked on her tea. ''Course you'll get something, my loveys, just you wait and see. "Horrible children" indeed.'

'Anyway, we've just got to get all the decorations up ready for Father Christmas so let's get working, then when Christmas Eve comes, you two have got to go to bed nice and early so that you are both sound asleep before he comes.' Charlie looked across at Mark and winked. 'Have a snooze, Mrs Dowers, I reckon you need it. I'll wash up the tea cups.'

By four o'clock the sitting room chairs were covered with paper chains and the children's excitement ran high.

'When can we put them up, Uncle Charlie? We've done ever such a lot, haven't we?'

'We'll do some more tomorrow, then we'll put them up, all three of us, Mark. Hope your mum will be able to come down next week, and we've got to get it all done by then. There's a Christmas tree to decorate too, so we'll have our work cut out to do it all.' Charlie picked Samantha up and carried her upstairs. When he put her down on the landing, she ran into the big bedroom.

'Mummy, Uncle Charlie says we're going to put the paper chains up soon. We've made ever such a lot.'

'Have you, little one?' Glenda looked at her daughter's happy face. What a wonderful sight, she thought. 'Charlie, you've made them so happy. When they are in bed, you must tell me what's been happening while I've lain here. They seem to have new clothes too. Where did they come from?'

'We'll talk later, Glenda,' Charlie said. 'First we are all going to have our tea and cakes. Come on, Mrs Dowers, let's help you with that lot and I'll bring some chairs up for us all.'

'Mummy, we've had such fun in the snow with Uncle Charlie. We've made a big snowman, and he's got a carrot stuck in his face for a nose. Uncle Charlie said that was the right thing to do,' Mark said, full of excitement. 'And we threw snowballs at each other. It's lovely here, Mum. Can we call Mrs Dowers "Nanny", Mum, 'cos she's ever so nice?'

'Oh, go on with you, Mark.' Mrs Dowers was blushing. 'But you can call me Nanny, love, that's lovely.'

'Nanny Dowers,' Glenda said. 'You are like a mother, you know, and you have been to me. We think you're lovely, don't we, children?'

'We love her, Mummy,' said Mark, 'and we want to stay here always. We can, can't we?'

'You can and will,' Charlie said. 'Don't worry about that, laddie. No one is going to take you away from your mother.' Charlie put down the chairs he had carried in. 'Come on then, tuck in, and you, Glenda, we've got to fatten you up for Christmas. Next week we will get you downstairs for a while each day and by Christmas Day you should be about ready to enjoy it.'

Later that evening while the children slept and Mrs Dowers had gone next door to her home, Charlie and Glenda talked. He told her about Mrs Dowers, or Nanny Dowers as she was now called, getting the clothes for the children and her. He assured her they were stocked with everything they needed to see them over the next few weeks. Then he told her he had put his house up for sale, leaving it with an agent to deal with because he would stay here with the three of them. 'There's no way I'd leave you alone to cope, love, no way at all.' Doctor Evans had advised against him leaving her, because she would take a long time to get really well.

'Oh Charlie, what would we have done without you? You know I love you, don't you, but I can't go any further than we are now. I'm so sorry, love, forgive me, but I can't do it.'

'I don't expect anything of you, or from you, Glenda. You need a lot of time to get over the trauma of all those years. When you feel ready you'll know and tell me. I'll wait. You have given me the one thing I never had, and that's a family. Not all men are like your husband, you know. Some of us do believe a woman, especially our wife, is something special. I think of you as my wife already and we don't have to sleep together to prove it, love. You'll know when you are ready, don't worry about it. Anyway, we have to get your divorce settled first and the custody of the children. When you feel fit, perhaps when the new year comes, we can go into it with my solicitor, but we won't think about that yet. Christmas is to be enjoyed first.'

'Charlie, oh Charlie, don't ever leave here, there would be no life without you around.' Glenda felt the tears stinging her eyes and she struggled to control herself. 'There's money in my purse that you should have to help pay for all the things you have bought, and Nanny Dowers should have extra for all her work. I haven't got much but you take what's there.'

'Now that's something you don't have to worry about. I told you before, I don't have any money worries. I've got money from my business sale, it will be quite enough for our needs. When the house is sold, that will be put in trust for you and the children so that you will always be secure should anything happen to me, though I can't see that happening, seeing that we won't be going anywhere, except maybe on holiday when the divorce and custody of the children are settled.'

'You don't think the courts will allow him access to them, do you, Charlie? He never wanted them around him before and I can't see why he should now, but he would apply for it just to make things awkward. They're terrified of him so I doubt if they would go anyway.'

'Love, when the courts hear how he treated you and them, I doubt he'll be allowed near them. You know, while you were lying here, Dr Evans and Nurse Libby talked to them both and they say they have never had children so frightened of their father before. They spent a long time with them but I don't know what they asked, and neither Mark nor Samantha would talk about it except to keep asking me not to send them back home to their daddy. Mark said, "I hate him because he hit Mummy and made her so ill" and his little face was really bitter. I'm glad you didn't see it, it would have upset you too much.'

'Harry never did like them around him, and when they were, on the odd occasion, he did nothing but yell at them and tell them to go to their rooms. He didn't hit them though or that would have been the final straw for me. I would have killed him, Charlie, I would have.' Glenda felt the tears running down her cheeks, and it seemed like a dam had burst. She reached out for him and he held her gently. Her body was racked with sobs which she didn't seem able to stop.

Mark woke up and seeing his mother crying was out of bed in a flash. 'What's the matter with Mummy?' he asked, full of alarm.

'She's just crying out all her bad feelings, Mark. She will feel better when she has.' Charlie put an arm around him and pulled him close.

After a while, Glenda quietened down, but still her body shook with sobs. 'Mark,' she said through her sobs, 'go back to bed, love, you'll get cold.'

'No, he won't. He's going to sit by you in your bed so move over. He'll watch you and I'll go and make us all a nice hot drink – cocoa, I think, don't you, Mark?'

'Yes, Uncle Charlie, that's lovely. Move over, Mummy, and I'll get in the bed.'

'Be careful, Mark, your mum's still very sore son, go gentle.'

'Oh, I will, Uncle Charlie. You and me have to make her well, don't we?'

'Sure thing,' said Charlie as he went through the door. At least she's had a good cry now, he thought, so the healing of the emotional scars should start now. Dear God, what a life she's had. Why do you leave beasts like that, Lord, and take my Laura who was so good? But there was no answer.

Chapter Seventeen

The paper chains were all up, and the tree was ablaze with lights and tinsel. Glenda was coming down today for the first time, and the children were bursting with the excitement of it all.

Nanny Dowers had made the mince pies specially for today, and they would all sit round the Parkray boiler in the sitting room for their elevenses. The fire was a bright red glow showing through the glass.

The door opened and Glenda, helped by Charlie, walked slowly into the room.

'Wow,' she said. 'You *have* been busy, haven't you?'

'We made all the chains, Mummy,' said Samantha, 'and then we did the tree. Uncle Charlie said we had to get it all done for you today, so we worked and worked.'

'It looks lovely, and I think I'm a lucky mummy to have two clever children like you.'

Glenda was put into a chair padded well with pillows, near the fire. Nanny Dowers bustled in with tea and mince pies.

'Now, let's all tuck in before they get cold. Made them special this morning.'

Nurse Libby was still coming in every day to dress the scalds Glenda had; her face had now lost most of its puffiness. The stitches had been taken out of her face but there was still the redness over her cheeks and nose. Glenda hoped the scars would not show too much and that the redness would soon go. It didn't matter that her body would bear the marks of ill treatment, but she did worry about her face. Where the stitches had been was still swollen and very sore right inside.

There was a contented silence as they ate the mince pies and drank their tea. The fire looked cheerful, and Glenda thought she had never before known such contentment.

'Nanny Dowers, you're such a lovely cook,' she said. 'You've done so much for us I don't know how to thank you. You've been like a mother to me, and you feel like my mother. You're the one I never knew or had, and I bless you.'

'I've only done what any decent person would have done. Anyway, lovey, we had to get you well, didn't we? Your children are a credit to you, so it's not all one-sided. Now let's clear these things away, children, and then we'll have to see about dinner. It's chops, chips and peas today, how about that?'

'Coo, lovely,' said Mark, jumping up to help. 'Come on, Sam, let's help.'

When they had all left the room, Charlie said, 'Mrs Dowers is looking after all their presents 'til Christmas Eve. When you are better you'll be able to go out and meet the people here. You'll like them, they are friendly but not overpowering, and will help anyone in trouble. They were very good to me and my wife when she was ill. I used to bring her here until it got too much for her.'

'I hope you haven't spent too much on them. They really are not used to it. One present only is all they were ever allowed and that's only because it came out of the housekeeping. Charlie, you really are spoiling them.'

'Why not?' he said. 'That's what children are for at Christmas, to spoil. Wait until you see their presents. There's some for the pillowcases and then some for the tree and some more for Boxing Day. They may not always get so many, but this year yes, there is a lot of making up to do.'

Christmas Eve came. The children had gone to bed quietly, but they were full of excitement. Never before had they known such a fuss over Christmas. All previous Christmases had bad memories attached because by the time it was over, Daddy had had one of his rages and Mummy was ill again.

'Will this one be all right, Mark?' Samantha asked when they were in bed.

'I think so, Sam. Uncle Charlie isn't like Daddy, you know. Anyway, we'd better go to sleep before Mummy comes up. She'll be here in a minute.'

'Goodnight, Mark, God bless.' Samantha snuggled down the bed next to Mark.

'God bless, Samantha,' he said, putting his arm over her. 'Sleep well.'

When she was asleep, Mark said softly, 'Please, God, let this Christmas be nice for us all. Don't let anything spoil it. Look after Mummy and Uncle Charlie and Nanny Dowers, please, God.' With that he drifted off to sleep.

Glenda was now able to dress and undress herself without too much trouble. She wore only trousers and a jumper that buttoned in the front so it wasn't too difficult. Her night-dress was big and easy to get on and off, as were all her clothes at present.

When she was ready, Charlie helped her into bed and, tucking her in, kissed the top of her head. 'You go to sleep now and I'll bring in the pillowcases we got ready,' he whispered. 'I'll see to the tree presents, so don't you worry. Goodnight, love, sleep well.'

He crept out and into his bedroom and carried in the pillowcases, one by one, putting them on either side of the double bed. Looking over to Glenda, he saw that she was already asleep, and creeping back to his room he collected a third pillowcase, filled to the brim like the others. This he put at the foot of Glenda's bed on the floor. Each one had a name tag on it so they wouldn't get mixed up. He then crept down the stairs and went to Mrs Dowers to collect the tree presents.

When they had spread them around the tree, they sat and drank tea together and talked about what was to be done on Christmas Day. The turkey was cooked ready and the vegetables all done. All he had to do was cook them. The pudding was ready in the steamer and he just had to light the gas under it.

'Think you'll manage?' Mrs Dowers asked. 'There's a lot to do, or do you want me to come in?'

'No, Nanny, you've done enough. You go to your daughter and enjoy yourself. I could never have done all this without your help, all the presents and everything. You've been an angel.'

'You'll have me sprouting wings soon,' Nanny replied. 'I'm off. Early start tomorrow to help my daughter. See you after Christmas then, but you know where I am if you want me. Goodnight, happy Christmas.' So saying, she left, shutting the door quietly behind her.

I'd better get to bed too, he thought. There'll be a lot of goings-on tomorrow.

Charlie was woken up by the shrieks from the front bedroom. He looked at the clock. Six o'clock! Well, I'd better get up and make a start, he thought. Before he could get out of bed, his door was pushed open and two little people fell over his bed.

'Uncle Charlie, he came!' Samantha shouted. 'Father Christmas came, and brought ever such a lot of presents, do come and see.'

They were tugging him out of bed, and he had a struggle to put on his dressing gown as he went into their room.

'Look at this, and this,' they were shouting at him.

'Oh my, you have been lucky, haven't you,' he said. 'But I see another one over there. Who is that one for?'

They looked to where he pointed and jumped off their bed to get it.

'It's for Mummy,' yelled Mark. 'Mummy, look, it's for you.'

Glenda looked at Charlie and couldn't speak.

'Undo it, Mummy, let's see what you have,' Samantha said, trying to lift the pillowcase up.

Mark helped her to put it on the bed, and Glenda leaned forward. Never before had she had so many gifts, clothing, perfume, so many things.

'Charlie, oh Charlie, you're wonderful. What a Christmas for us all. Children, go and see what we have hidden in the wardrobe.'

'Ooh yes,' Mark said, dashing to the wardrobe. He brought out three packages. 'These are for you, Uncle Charlie, from us,' he said solemnly, 'because we love you.'

'Open them, Uncle Charlie.' Samantha was jumping up and down in her excitement.

'Right then.' Charlie sat down to do the opening of their presents. There was a pullover, a shirt and gloves and a scarf.

'Smashing,' he said. 'I've never had it so good. Think I'll go and make some tea, then we've got to get dressed and take in Nanny Dowers' presents before she goes out to her daughter, so let's get cracking. You two go and wash and dress yourselves, don't forget to wash behind your ears, and you can put on the new things we bought for today. See you in a minute.'

An hour later, they crept to Nanny Dowers' house and knocked on the door. When she opened it, they all shouted, 'Happy Christmas, Nanny.'

'Come in, all of you, out of the cold. What's all this then?'

'For you, Nanny, from all of us,' Samantha shouted. Open them, they're special for you.'

'Oh well, I'd better get on with it, hadn't I?' As she opened them, the children were jumping around her in their excitement. 'Oh my, look at all of this. Well I never, such a lot of things. What a Christmas, well dear me now.' She hugged Mark and Samantha to her. 'You enjoy your day, loveys. Be good, children, and help Uncle Charlie because he's got a lot to do.'

'Oh we will, Nanny,' said Mark. 'I wish he was our daddy, he's ever so kind.'

'That I know, love,' Nanny replied. 'I've known him a long time and a nicer man you couldn't find.'

'Hold on, all of you, you'll make me blush. Anyway, I don't have anyone else to be nice to, do I, so I've made you my family now. Anyway, young 'uns, we've got to get cracking. We've got dinner to cook, you know, and your mum to see to when Nurse Libby's been. So come on, and let Nanny get to her daughter's.'

'We love you, Nanny. Have a nice day. Wish you were going to be with us.' Mark hugged her and Samantha kissed her cheek.

'Go on, you two, off you go and help Mummy and Uncle Charlie.'

When Nurse Libby came, they gave her a present too with the children jumping around her.

'Well, such a change in the children since I first saw you,' she said.

'You should see all our presents, Nurse,' said Mark, grinning at Samantha. 'Father Christmas left us ever such a lot.'

'Did he now, then he must have known how nice you both are, mustn't he? See you tomorrow, enjoy yourselves, and thank you very much.' As she left she was very thoughtful. I bet they have never had a Christmas like it, probably always been kept subdued. Do hope everything goes all right and they can stay, without any further stress. Still, if my report is fully understood, it should all work out.

'Right then, you go upstairs and tidy up and help your mother, and I'll get the dinner started, then we can have breakfast.' Charlie shooed them up the stairs. First the fire to see to, then the food. First things first. As he started his work he could hear Glenda talking quietly upstairs, and the children answering. Bet they've never been so free, he thought.

Chapter Eighteen

1956–1964

Harry came back on the stroke of ten o'clock. He slammed the front door and strode into the dining room. When he saw the meat and vegetables with the broken dishes lying where he had thrown them, he thought he would burst. He also noticed among the debris a tea towel, wet and red.

'What did I tell you, woman?' he yelled, as he went up the stairs three at a time.

He got to the bedroom door and saw Glenda's bloodstained clothes lying on the floor with bits of vegetables sticking to them. He went toward the bed and checked, realising it was empty.

Raging, he went into the children's room, and finding it empty, it penetrated his mind that the house was silent. 'Where the bloody hell are you, slut?' he shrieked. 'You think you can hide from me?'

Going from room to room, he found the same, even looking into the cupboard under the stairs. I bet she's gone round to that daft sister of mine, he thought. Well, she'll soon be back here, I'll see to that.

His mind in a turmoil of rage, he charged out of the house and through the streets until he reached the house where his sister Monica lived. He hammered on the knocker, and with his fist, on the door.

'Who is it? What's all the racket?' From inside, the lights started going on.

'It's Harry, who else? Open the door before I break it down, come on, you fool.'

As Monica opened the door he pushed it back violently, and charged passed her, knocking her against the wall. 'Where is she, eh, where is she? What's she doing, eh, hiding in some corner thinking I won't find her? Come on, slut, out, you're going home.'

'What are you on about, man? Have you gone mad?'

'Gone mad? Me? You bring out that stupid wife of mine, go on, bring her here.'

'Glenda? Isn't she home?' Monica looked at her brother's face. It was red and angry just like he used to be when a child in one of his tantrums.

'Would I be here if she was at home? You're about as daft as she is. Just get her in here, no more messing about.'

'Well, she's not here, you can search the place if you like, but don't touch anything or I'll have the police on you so quick you won't know what's hit you. This is my house, not yours, and just you remember it.'

Harry flung her to one side and raced through each room. He knew them well enough, for this was where he'd lived before he'd gone into the army. Now his sister owned it. Mum would have known what to do if she were alive, she always had, whatever he'd done, she'd always made things right. Why did you bloody die, Mum? You should be here to help me. He had always had this inner rage against life and could only get relief by doing something violent to someone or something.

When he came back to Monica, she said, 'Well, are you satisfied? She's not here, and if I did know where she was I wouldn't tell you. I'd have left you long ago, little brother, or killed you, one or the other.'

'I'll find her, and God help her when I do, she'll regret walking out on me. Bloody place is a mess, and who will clean that up, I'd like to know.'

'You will, little brother, there's nobody else now, is there? Now get out and don't come round here again. You sicken me. Clear off.'

Monica strode to the front door and flung it open. 'If you come back here, I'll get the police on you, so don't try it. I've got my own life to live and that does not include you, ever. You made my life a hell on Earth when we were kids, no way are you going to do so now. You're on your own, boy. Bugger off and stay there.' As he went through the door she slammed it shut.

So she's left him at last, good for her. Wonder where she's gone though. Must have had a fancy man up her sleeve all the time. Good luck to her, poor little sod. Laughing to herself, she made some tea, and drinking it, found she was really enjoying the thought of Harry having to look after himself, something he'd never done in his life before.

Perhaps if she could have seen a little into the future, things would not have pleased her so much, but then how many of us know what the future holds?

On the way home, with his thoughts raging in his mind, Harry thought what he would do to Glenda when she came back. It didn't occur to him that she wouldn't come back. He savoured the thought of feeling his hands punching her all over. She was his wife, wasn't she, and he could do what he liked with her. He grinned as he walked along. What were women for, anyway? They were there to pleasure a man, that's what they were for, that's what Mum always said.

He noticed that in front of him was a girl walking alone, her high heels tapping the pavement as she walked. Quickening his pace, he came up behind her, and as she turned, he grabbed her by the coat and punched her in the face. As she fell to the ground, he kicked her, not caring where his boot went. She just lay there, and seeing her blood-spattered body lying so still, it penetrated his mind that he'd better get going before somebody came along. He started running and didn't stop until he reached his own road. That's one for you, you bitch, he thought, seeing her in his mind as Glenda.

When he got in he went straight to the bedroom, and, feeling much calmer now, he searched for a bag to put Glenda's clothes in. Must clear this up, got to go to work tomorrow. Don't want this lot to come home to.

Then he went downstairs and got a cloth from the kitchen, and newspaper. He got on his knees and started wiping all the food off the floor. Wrapping it up, he went out to the dustbin, and put in the bag of clothes and paper parcel of food. By God, she'll suffer for making me do this, he thought. If she's not back in two days, I'll go to the police and report her missing. When they've found her she'll regret what she's done.

As he got undressed he realised his clothes were splashed with blood. Have to sponge this off, he thought, and then get them laundered. I'll cut my face tomorrow shaving and say that's where the blood came from. Daft cleaners will believe anything. Then he stood for a while. No, better cut my hand and bandage it up, that'll be a better idea. You get more blood from a cut hand than from a shaving cut.

Having made his decision, he got into bed and went to sleep with a smile on his face. His last thought as he drifted off was to think of what he would do to Glenda when she returned. After all, where could she go with two children and no family to help her? His dreams were muddled, but he remembered them clearly when he awoke next morning. His mother was there, telling him as she had when he was a child that it didn't matter what he did as long as he got pleasure from it, but behind her there was Monica and a policeman saying that they were waiting for him, it was only a matter of time before he would get his just desserts. He awoke, shouting at them, 'I can do as I like. I always have, haven't I? Mum said I could, so why did they try to interfere? Mind your own business and clear off.' They all faded into the distance, but the policeman pointed to his watch and said, 'We'll get you in time, laddie, we'll wait.'

He found he was sweating, and felt the familiar anger starting to build up inside him. The dreams like these were coming more often now, and he didn't like them one bit. After all, why should the police want him? What he did in his own home was his business, wasn't it?

When he saw his blood-spattered overcoat and trousers in a heap on the chair where he'd left them the night before, he remembered that he had decided to cut his hand. I wonder why, he thought. He knew that Glenda and the kids were not there, but remembered nothing else except going round to see Monica. She's always hated me, always been jealous because Mum loved me more than her. Well, sod her, I don't need her. He grinned when he thought back to the times when Monica had been curled up in her bed crying because his mum had given her a good welting for something he'd done. Mum always believed anything he said. I could lie the back teeth off a donkey, he thought.

Oh Mum, why did you have to die? Of his father he thought nothing, he was just a shadowy figure, always shouting and pushing them around or hitting out with his fists. 'Good job when he went' was always his feeling towards him.

He looked at his hand and began to plan how he would cut it. He knew he had to do this to give a reason for all the blood on his clothes, but he did not know why. Couldn't be because of Glenda because she wasn't there, was she? I wonder why, but still, must get on with it. Better wash and dress first, or I'll be spoiling another lot of clothes.

When he'd dressed and had his breakfast, such as it was, he searched through the kitchen drawer to find a sharp-pointed knife. He raged within. All her fault. If she was here I wouldn't have to do this. By God she'd pay when she came back.

He found a small sharp pointed knife and stood there, looking from it to his hand. What would he be doing to make him cut his hand? Potatoes, yes potatoes, and the knife could slip, yes, that was it. Having decided, he got out a potato and rinsed it under the tap. Taking hold of the knife, he started to peel it and, with one stroke, cut his thumb from the top down to the wrist and then across the base of the palm. As the blood spurted out he thought, Yes, that ought to do it. It seemed to him there was enough blood around to account for the clothes upstairs. Without cleaning the sink where he'd dropped the knife and potato, he rinsed his hand under the tap, wrapped a tea towel round it, and went up to the bathroom. He couldn't find any kind of dressing there big enough to cover the long cut he'd made. Bloody useless woman, never has anything I want. Back to the kitchen he went and, wrapping a fresh tea towel round his hand, he put on the overcoat hanging on the hall stand, checked he had got his key, and made his way to the hospital.

By the time he reached there, the towel was soaked with blood, and the sight of it made him feel good. A lovely colour, he thought. The casualty doctor put in some stitches, and a nurse bandaged his hand. 'You're going to have a job washing with one hand,' she said, as she jabbed him in the arm with a needle, and he again felt anger rising within him. None of this would be necessary, would it, if that slut of his was where she belonged.

Chapter Nineteen

The week passed slowly with Harry getting what food he could. Bloody woman, he thought. How does she expect me to do everything with one hand? Self-pity and anger fought a raging battle within him. He'd collected his clothes from the cleaner's, and they were hanging in the wardrobe.

The girl in the cleaner's was very sympathetic when she saw the bandage on his hand. 'Must be very painful,' she had said, but Harry hadn't felt any pain in his hand, his pain was the anger within him.

He had been to the police on Wednesday, and although they had appeared to show concern, their main concern was for the children. 'We'll put out a bulletin and see if anything comes from it,' they had said. When asked what he had done to his hand he'd said he did it peeling potatoes, which he wasn't used to doing, and the officer had laughed and said, 'Yes, mate, must be a problem looking after yourself. I'd make a right hash of it.'

Stupid bugger, Harry thought as he went home. Bet he'd make a hash of anything. They're all as daft as brushes. Couldn't catch a flea on a dog. His dream flashed back into his mind and he shivered, but didn't know why.

He'd telephoned where he worked and told his boss he wouldn't be in this week because of his hand. 'Couldn't work machinery like that,' his boss agreed.

On Friday, the local paper was put through his letter-box. On the front page was the headline: 'Young girl found battered'. He saw before his eyes a young girl walking along the road in the dark, and heard her heels clicking on the pavement. He shook his head and read on:

> *Young girl found battered by passer-by in the late hours of last Sunday. She was taken to hospital and is reported to be in a stable condition.*
> *Injuries to her face and body are severe, but robbery or sexual assault does not appear to be a motive,' said the police officer in charge of the incident. Police are asking for any witnesses to come forward. A full investigating team has been set up to deal with the crime.*

As he read it, Harry felt a great deal of satisfaction. That's another stupid bitch dealt with, he thought, but the knowledge that he had been the attacker did not register. He put the paper down and leaned back in the armchair. Already the house was untidy, for he didn't bother with housework. Better get washed up in the kitchen or there won't be anything left to use.

Washing up, like everything else, was difficult with one hand, even though he only had his breakfast and the odd drink at home; his main meal he went to pubs or cafés for. As he swirled the cups and plates around in the water, he felt a sudden burst of anger against Glenda for leaving him when he needed her. He could only use one hand, couldn't he, so what was she thinking of, going off at a time like this? Some wife!

Damn, won't be able to play golf this weekend because of her. Still, I'll go down to the club and get a bit of company. Not that he spoke to many people. Their conversation is so stupid, he thought. They talk of nothing but their wives and kids, and their great business deals. Still, he would go there and probably take a walk over the course, even if he couldn't play. Bit of fresh air, that's what I need, he thought.

As the weekend wore on, he felt the anger rising in him, and at six o'clock on Sunday, when he should have come home to a meal, his anger and hunger were rampant within him. He slammed the front door shut, and went to his usual pub, got a drink and sat in a corner away from the noise. No one spoke to him because the angry look on his face kept everyone at a distance. At ten o'clock he left and walked through the back streets before turning for home. There were a few people about and they were groups or couples. His self-pity made him feel he was going to burst.

As he turned a corner he saw before him a woman alone. In his mind she was Glenda. He raced up to her, took hold of her shoulder, and swung her round.

'Bitch, slut, you should be at home where you belong!' And as he shrieked these words his fist crashed into her face. Blood spurted from her nose and mouth and she crumpled to the ground. As she did so, she put up her arms to defend her head. He kicked her wherever he could get his boot. 'That's the way to deal with you,' he growled, then, hearing footsteps running towards them, he realised the need to escape. Running until he was out of breath, he finally turned into his own road. Thankfully, he let himself in at the door and went to the kitchen.

Still panting, but feeling very pleased with himself, Couldn't catch me, he thought. He heard the distant sound of an ambulance bell. That's got her where she belongs, hope she rots in hell.

'Another Woman Attacked.' Harry read the headline. He was still unable to work and found that time dragged in the house on his own. He'd gone round to see Monica but she told him to, 'Clear off. I'm not going to help you. I had enough of you years ago.'

He read on and learned that the police were connecting the attack on this woman with the one the previous week. 'Probably committed by the same man. No evident motive.'

Bet if I attacked a few more women as well, that would stump them, he thought. He did not remember getting rid of the bloodstained clothing when he had come home the previous Sunday evening.

I'd have to wear something I could sponge down though, or the cleaner's will be asking questions, must avoid any suspicion falling on me. Yes, that would be a way of getting my own back on that bitch of mine. Must start working things out, and be clever about it. He grinned to himself and sat working out ways of outwitting the police and where he could go to attack women, without the risk of anyone coming along. Prostitutes, yes, that could be one way. They take you back to their own place. Of course, I could get my satisfaction and then give them what for. Wouldn't cost me a penny then.

The rest of the day, his thoughts revolved around the serious business, to him, of how he would carry out the attacks. Better be picked up in the street, not a pub, or I might be recognised. I'll go further afield, that's an idea, and of course if I haven't got any clothes on I won't have to worry because there won't be any bloodstained clothes to worry about. He laughed loud and long with the sheer joy of thinking what he would do. He didn't decide on a day, he would just take any chance that came. They'll be going round in circles. He pictured the police, masses of them, going round and round asking their questions and getting nowhere. From self-pity his feelings had changed to complete happiness, feeling full of pride at his cleverness.

The following week the headline read: 'When are the police going to act?' Two more women had been attacked, both in their own homes, one was so seriously injured it was doubtful if she would live.

Harry read the paper and felt so pleased with himself he could not remain in his chair. He strode around the room remembering and savouring each attack. What silly bitches they were. Any woman who took a strange man home just for sex deserved to be punished, and he was the man to do it. So one might die? Well, that would be one less whore in the community. I'm cleaning the place up, that's what I'm doing. God's work, that's it. Can't let women like that go on living.

He decided he would go out again and really finish one of the prostitutes off in about a week's time. If I can clear this area of them then I'll start somewhere else, get rid of them all. Never know, I might come across that wife of mine. How else could she be living anyway? She'd got no one to go to.

Of his children he thought not at all. They did not exist, only him and Glenda, and if he continued to do what he had started he would be doing everyone a good turn. Dirty bitches, they have to be exterminated, nothing else for it.

Christmas passed, and the New Year came. By the end of January, three more women had been attacked. Harry decided he must go further afield in his efforts. He travelled by bus or underground north and south of the Thames, striking whenever he had the opportunity. Sometimes it might be a woman walking alone in a street, and sometimes a prostitute in her own home. He got more satisfaction when dealing with a prostitute, for his sexual appetite was sated too. He would sometimes have to walk home many miles, but as he felt so good within himself that did not matter.

The second week in February, a large letter was delivered through his letter-box. Can't be a bill, they are small letters. When he read the contents he thought he would burst, so angry did he become. Divorce? Her divorce me, how dare she? The grounds for the petition for divorce were stated as persistent cruelty. In addition she wanted total and complete control and custody of the children. If he made any attempt to contest the divorce or gain custody of the children she would sue him in court for grievous bodily harm. No address was given for Glenda, only the address of the solicitor. It stated that the solicitor had sufficient evidence to prove his abuse of his wife on one particular occasion, and also over a long period. In addition he had evidence of mental abuse concerning the children. Proceedings for a court hearing were currently in hand.

Harry sat, stunned. What were they on about? She was his wife, wasn't she? Nobody could interfere between man and wife. He could do as he liked. She was his property, wasn't she? As far as the kids were concerned he couldn't give a toss. Anyway, if he had the kids he wouldn't be able to carry on his crusade, and clean the streets of prostitutes, would he?

How dare she do this? Who was behind her, eh? Someone must be, you couldn't go for a divorce with no money. Oh, he would find them one day and deal with the fancy man, oh yes he would. He savoured the thought. Would have to be careful though, in case the chap was built like an all-in wrestler, but he would find a way, even if he waited years.

The anger began to mount up within him. By the time night fell he was ready to set forth to deal with another bitch woman and hoped he would be able to find one tonight, nothing else could or would cool this burning within him. It was too early to go out yet though, have to wait until about seven o'clock, and then travel. Where to tonight? Maybe he would go further north in London, he would see. Going south of the Thames took time, and he wanted satisfaction as soon as possible.

By now the national newspapers were reporting the attacks on women. None of them would die but most would be scarred for life, mentally and physically. Serve them right, dirty lot.

What Harry did not know was that time was running out for him. With the descriptions of their attacker given to the police by the women in the street and the prostitutes, an artist's impression had been made and circulated to all Metropolitan forces, and a further shock was in store for Harry.

The evening paper was delivered. He made a cup of tea and sat down to enjoy it, thinking of his night's work ahead. When he opened the paper, there before him was a face so like his own, he shook in his chair. 'Wanted by the police.'

It can't be me they want. I'm helping them, doing their job for them, the fools. His anger against the police knew no bounds. How dare they interfere with his mission in life. They're getting at me all roads round, what with Glenda and her damned divorce, then this. His recurrent dream flashed before his eyes. He saw Monica and the policeman clearly, and the policeman was really smiling now. 'Time's up,' he said.

Damn you, he thought. You won't get me, I'll go elsewhere and start again. You can all go to hell. He went upstairs and started packing his suitcase. Trying to get everything in was a job, there seemed to be so much. In his haste he had thrown everything in the case in a heap. Take it all out and start again, he thought. Don't want to leave anything that could be useful. Knives, yes, I'll want knives, they might come in very useful. He dashed to the kitchen and picked up two of the sharpest knives he could find, and was halfway up the stairs when there was a knock at the door. He hesitated, didn't know whether to go up or down. Go up and get the suitcase and go out the back way, that's it. I'll climb out of the bathroom window on to the lean-to, then I'll be off.

The door knocker was banged more loudly and a voice said, 'Police, open up.' Harry turned towards the front door. 'Sod you, you stupid buggers!' And he ran to the bedroom, grabbed hold of his case, and ran to the bathroom. Opening the window quietly, he climbed out. He had not thought of the slope of the lean-to roof or the snow and ice. As he put his feet out, they slid beneath him and down, down he went, to fall to the ground. He still had the knives in his hand and as he fell, one penetrated his chest. Furious with the pain and his own stupidity, he shrieked, cursing everyone and everything to hell.

'Delivered to us nicely, I think,' a voice said. Looking up, he saw the hefty form of a police sergeant and standing by him was a younger one. 'Put the cuffs on, lad,' said the big man. 'Don't think he's going far, do you?' As Harry made a move to rise, his chest seared with pain, and he found he was unable to stand any pressure on one leg. He found that the leg was scorching out pain too. His hands were grasped firmly and the handcuffs put on.

'Bastards, you bastards, get your filthy hands off me.' And as he spoke he felt he was drowning in spittle. He spat it out and saw that it was red. Only then did it dawn on him that he was hurt, and fear overtook him. 'Help me, do something, can't you?' Tears as well as blood were choking him now.

'Get the ambulance, lad, and tell the Inspector I need him here, go on then. Quickly.'

Chapter Twenty

Harry stood in the dock of the court, facing the judge. The jury had returned to the court and given the verdict: 'Guilty.'

The judge looked sternly at him. Harry stared back, unblinking. What were they doing finding him guilty? He'd done a good job of ridding the place of whores. They should be standing here, not him. The judge's words barely penetrated his muddled brain, and anyway he didn't agree with what he was saying, so why should he listen to that old fool?

'You have been found guilty on four charges of grievous bodily harm. Taking into account the psychiatric reports, I have to pass a sentence which will protect society from you. The crimes you have been found guilty of are the most brutal I have had to deal with. The injuries sustained by your victims will disfigure and affect them for the rest of their lives, indeed they were lucky to survive. I therefore sentence you to be detained for an indefinite period in a secure institution suitable for your needs. I further recommend you should never be allowed your freedom.'

The judge stood, bowed to the court, and left. As Harry turned to leave, handcuffed to two prison officers, he saw Monica. There was a satisfied smirk on her face and he tried to turn back to shout out what he thought of her, but the officers jerked him forward down the steps of the dock, and to the cells below. They led him into a small room below the court where he waited for his solicitor. When he came, Harry was ready for him.

'Bloody fat lot of good you did, you daft sod. Why should I have been found guilty, when I was doing society a service?'

'Hold it, mate,' one of the officers said. 'Mind your language. Your solicitor has come to see what else he can do for you, concerning your personal affairs.'

'That's a joke. If he makes as good a job of that as he has this, I'll be in dead trouble.'

Mr Jakes, his solicitor, sat down opposite him with a table between them. 'I've come to see if you want me to sell your house for you or if I can help in any other way.'

'Sell my house, why should I? Bought that outright I did, with my gratuity money, and some money my mum left me. No, you get it let and I'll have the income from it. No one's going to have that house but me. I'll be free one day and I'll need it. You make sure it's kept up to scratch, I want it looked after.' Harry thought to himself, They must be mad to think they can keep me in jail for good.

The prison officers and solicitor looked at each other, but said nothing.

'Then there is your divorce. I don't think you will get far by contesting that now. Just let it go through, man, it will anyway. You'll be wasting your time and money fighting it.'

'Do what you bloody like about that. I wouldn't have her back on a silver platter now, the dirty bitch. She's nothing but a slut.' The anger was rising in Harry and seeing this, the senior officer signalled to Mr Jakes to leave. He knew only too well how violent Harry could become when angry. If his poor little devil of a wife had had to put up with it for years it was no wonder she was divorcing him. Inspector Barbrum came into the room.

'Right, men, let's get him moved, shall we? The sooner the better.'

Everything that had happened since his arrest was a blur in Harry's mind. He remembered being in hospital, and knew he'd had an operation because his chest was strapped up. They had to remove part of one lung, but when they told him, it didn't mean anything to him except that there was a damned uncomfortable tube stuck in his chest. One wrist was handcuffed to a cot side. Fancy putting me in a cot, like a baby, he had fumed within. In the other arm there was a tube with blood running through it. He liked watching that because blood was a lovely colour, but when they changed that to a clear fluid he became very angry and had to be sedated. He was a great trial to the staff, and always had two prison officers with him. Bloody sods never speak to me, and the self-pity and anger were always present.

He vaguely remembered various men coming in to talk to him, but did not really understand why they were asking such daft questions or who they were, only that they were doctors.

As soon as he was fit enough to move they had shifted him to another ward. He did not realise that it was a ward within a prison. He raged whenever he was awake, because he was still in a cot, and was still handcuffed to the side. Whenever he showed the least sign of starting to get violent, somebody came along and stuck a needle in him. 'Bloody assault, I call it,' he had said. 'I'll sue the lot of you.' But they always went away without saying a word.

He had to take a lot of tablets every day, and sometimes still had an injection. Whenever his solicitor came, he raged at him to get him released. 'What am I doing here anyway?' he always asked. Harry understood nothing of the charges brought against him, couldn't understand how they could be so daft as to charge him with these attacks on women. After all, he was only doing what any decent person would do, he was getting rid of filth from the streets.

When the charges and injuries had been read out in the court, he had smiled, for he remembered each one in detail. It thrilled him to see the women he had so brutally beaten sitting in or near the witness box giving their evidence. What a lovely job I did, he thought as he looked at their disfigurements. They won't be able to ply their trade in future. Only one was actually a prostitute but to Harry they all were.

One woman stated that her marriage was in trouble because her husband couldn't bear to look at her now. Her life was in ruins, she said. Good, so it ought to be, thought Harry, well pleased with himself. He studied her flattened nose.

Another, a girl of about eighteen, was in a wheelchair. It was stated that she would never walk again. When he had so brutally kicked her, he had broken her spine. He almost laughed aloud at that, so good it sounded. Smiling to himself, he sat calmly in the dock, and listened avidly, and as the dreadful injuries to each woman was revealed, he felt exultant. By God, I did a good job on that lot. They should have let me carry on, I'd have sorted out a lot more.

Members of the jury gasped when shown the photographs of the victims showing their appalling injuries. What's up with them, can't they stand the sight? Wish I could see them, that would make my day. But he was not able to see the photographs. All he could do to satisfy his lust for blood was to listen to every word each doctor said as they gave their evidence.

The ones he got angry with were those who stated that his mind was unsound, describing him as a person with a psychopathic disorder. If ever he were freed he would kill, because he was unable to differentiate between right and wrong.

'What did I do wrong?' he shouted. 'I helped clear the streets of whores, that's what I did. You should be thanking me.' At his outburst and violent waving of his arms, the judge ordered the court to be recessed, and Harry to be returned to the cells. As they took him out, he yelled, 'Bloody fools, you don't know a good bloke when you see one.' But down he had to go because the police officers were big, burly men, and soon controlled him. A doctor came in and gave him an injection which made him fuzzy in his mind, so that when he eventually went back into court, he couldn't really understand what was going on.

Now he was travelling in a police van to some place, but he didn't know where. See what it's like when I get there, he thought. If I don't like it, I'll leave.

But leave he did not. It finally dawned on him that he was to stay in this awful place, where there was no privacy, always someone watching you, where you couldn't stick your fist in anyone's face, without having a needle jabbed into you. He gradually came to accept that it was better to keep himself to himself, but from then on, planned how and when he would escape. There must be a way and I'll find it.

The days, weeks, months and years went by, all the same to Harry. He never had a visitor and did not want any, but always in his mind was the thought of revenge. It gradually came into his mind that the best person to go for would be the fancy man that bitch of his had gone off with. I'll get him, see if I don't. With this thought always in mind and never confided, he kept his mouth shut but his eyes and ears open. My chance will come.

And one day his chance did come. It required no planning, no skill, just chance and the luck of the draw. He had been detailed to do kitchen duties, and while the lorry driver collecting pigswill was busy lifting one of the bins, Harry swung up into the lorry and slithered along the floor to the front, where he could hide between the bins. The stench made him feel sick but all discomfort was sublimated to the need to get out so that he could do what he had to do for his own peace of mind, and that was to kill Glenda's fancy man.

Experience had taught him to keep the tumult of his emotions to himself. From the day he'd received his one and only letter in prison from his self-satisfied sister telling him about the happy family consisting of Glenda and that man, and a new baby, he had waited patiently for his chance. Oh, how his sister had crowed, rubbing it in about how happy Glenda and his children were, not that he cared about them, couldn't even remember what they looked like, but her, his wife, was nothing more than a common slut.

Oh yes, he had fooled them all in that place, so quietly had he behaved, daft lot, couldn't see what was before their eyes. They were all so pleased with him, they said. He'd wanted to spit obscenities at them but he had forced himself to sit calmly before them, but how he laughed at them. He was free!

I'll never go back, he vowed. I'll die first.

In his sock he had a lovely sharp knife which he'd whipped away when no one was looking. It's true, he thought, the more you behave as if butter wouldn't melt in your mouth, the more you can get away with. Daft buggers, they think they can read your mind but they can't. I'm too clever for them.

Harry raised his head and looked around. He saw they were travelling through the countryside, no buildings in sight.

Now's my chance, I'll pick the right spot then tip a couple of bins over, make a lot of noise about it so that he stops, then I'll nip away. If he tries to stop me, he'll know what for.

Chapter Twenty-One

He lay in the ditch listening for any sound that would tell him he'd been rumbled but there was nothing. So far, so good, but where to now? Got a hell of a way to go and I've got to get out of these stinking clothes.

His mind felt as sharp as a razor and he smiled to himself as he felt the knife in his sock. Lifting his head, he took stock of his position. Nothing but fields for miles. Got to get something to eat soon, and a drink, oh yes, a drink. In his pocket he had a few shillings but not enough to get him anywhere. In any case, he stank to high heaven, so fresh clothes were the first things to get. That bugger will pay for getting me like this, and through him, that bitch of a wife, if you could call her that, the whore.

He left his hiding place and walked along the field by the hedgerows, ducking down whenever he heard a car on the road. His greater problem was getting from field to field. After what seemed like hours, but was only two, he heard the sound of water flowing. It took a while to locate but then he found it over a rise in the ground.

He looked at the flow of the river and decided to go against it. The bank meandered to and fro interspersed with grassy bank and trees. I could bunk up here in the trees and be safe for a while. Daft fuzz will be checking the roads. Harry's problem was that he didn't know where he was, and the sooner he got clean clothes the better.

Coming towards him in the distance was a man riding a cycle, and as he got nearer Harry saw that he was elderly. All the better. Get him as he goes by. When the cyclist came abreast of him, he launched his attack, and as the man fell, he used his knife. Poor bugger didn't know what hit him.

He dragged the body into the cover of the trees, then got the bike. Strapped to the back was a mackintosh. Not bad, not bad at all. Harry stripped the man then stripped himself. Some minutes went by while he checked that there was no one around, then he dragged the man to the river bank and pushed him in. You've served your purpose, mate, sweet dreams. He watched the bubbles rise to the surface of the water and felt the thrill of a job well done. Now for me. He slipped into the water and swam to and fro then climbed out. Smell sweeter now, let's see what he had that I can wear.

Dressed and exhilarated with what he had accomplished, he cycled rapidly away. He was also richer now by a few pounds. Got paid for it too. And laughing loudly, he went on his way.

Luck remained with Harry, and in his journey over the next few days, he went through several small towns. In each one he mingled with the shoppers, and taking the opportunities as they arose, he managed to relieve a few women of their purses, which lay conveniently on top of their baskets. He wasn't greedy, and by the end of two weeks he had plenty of money for food and drink.

It could be said that the devil was looking after his own. He chose small cafés and small pubs in back streets. No one stopped him and no one spoke to him except to ask him what he wanted to eat and drink. By this time he had a fairly reasonable beard and a healthy tan. He slept where he could at night, in country hedgerows or old disused buildings. He used public toilets to wash in.

In two towns he gave himself a buzz by attacking lone women, but only to get their handbags, and by now he had a substantial sum of money. Of course, he didn't want to draw attention to himself, so he only acted when the coast was clear. Being small in stature, he gave the impression of being a younger man, but when on the cycle he appeared to be an old man. Harry was very resourceful and so very pleased with his beard. A good disguise, he chuckled to himself. At last he was on the outskirts of Gloucester. Nearly there, nearly there, his mind sang.

Three days later, he came to the village where Glenda lived, as she thought, in safety. Oh, you're safe, you dirty bitch, but he's not. Harry's mind clicked into overdrive. Got to go careful now, don't want to be inside again ever. Get the job done then we'll see where we go. So he planned his actions.

Mingle with the tourists, that's the thing to do. He still had enough money to see him through for a few more days. He left his cycle in the station car park and went in search of lodgings.

I'll come back for you soon, he thought as he clamped a lock round the wheels. Don't want anyone pinching it, some people would take the teeth from your head given the chance.

Two days later he was ready. He knew the woods where the fancy man went, and took himself there. When Charlie came in sight, he called a cheery 'Hello' to him. 'Nice woods these. There's nothing like a walk in the woods to refresh you, I always think.'

Charlie, in his innocence, bade him good day and agreed that there was peace and refreshment of the spirit to be found in woodland.

'I come here as often as I can. There are some lovely, quiet little pathways through the trees that people rarely use. They tend to stick to the main walks.'

Good, we won't be disturbed, thought Harry. He said to Charlie, 'I think they are afraid of losing their way.'

It was so easy and so neatly done. Charlie was chatting away amiably, while they walked deeper and deeper into the forest.

'I'll catch you up, something in my shoe,' he'd said to Charlie. 'Won't be a minute.'

Charlie continued on and suddenly felt a sharp pain in the back of his chest, then another, lower down. 'Oh God, what's that,' he said, as the blood pumped into his mouth. He fell to his knees, and, looking up at Harry, saw his face alight with demonic glee.

'Got you at last,' he spat at him, and plunged the knife in again and again. He left the knife sticking out of Charlie's chest. 'Thought you would live in sin, did you? Well, this is God's vengeance on you and I'm his Angel of Death.'

He was filled with delight. That's a good job done but I'd better make myself scarce. He took one last look at Charlie. Nobody would know you now, old sport, and nobody would want you now. Joy and peace seemed to fill him in equal measure. He was about to leave when he remembered he had little money left. Right, let's see what you have, mate. When he had finished, he was richer by a considerable amount. He tossed away the notes which were too bloodstained to use, and put the rest in his trouser pocket. Then he saw that his coat was badly stained with Charlie's blood. Get this off, no good to me now. He spent the next few minutes collecting fallen branches and some bracken and used it to cover his victim. Satisfied at last that he had covered the body as best he could, he made his way out of the woods, and by a roundabout way got back to his bike. By nightfall he was some thirty miles away, heading towards London.

It seemed to Harry that God had left everything he needed in his path, therefore He must be pleased with him. Like the jacket he had found on a seat in a pub car park, left there while the owner had gone back into the pub to fetch another drink. He'd found the jacket when he had stopped at the pub to use the gents and get a wash of sorts.

He heard in his mind, 'The devil looks after his own.' However, he rejected this and substituted, 'I'm doing God's work.' On and on he rode the bicycle, feeling elated as he pictured in his mind the blood flowing freely from that one's body. Even got your face, you bastard. That dirty bitch wouldn't want you now, would she, eh, would she?

When weariness forced him to rest, he lay sheltered in the lee of a hedge, and the next day continued on his way. He stopped for tea and a meal at a back street café in a small town on his journey, and continued this pattern until he reached his home town. His mind was playing tricks, he decided, because he thought he could see his sister and that policeman, and they were taunting him, 'It won't be long now,' but suddenly it wasn't his home town and they told him they had come to get him. 'Your time is up,' said the policeman, and Monica laughed and laughed.

'Get away from me,' his mind was yelling at them, but they always replied, 'No, we're here to stay, you have nowhere to go now, Harry.'

He left the bike propped against a wall a few streets away from his old home, and made the last part of the journey on foot. His mind was clear about his house. He knew he would have to break in, and he wanted the place to himself.

When at last he was in the house he had shared with Glenda, curiosity got the better of him. He walked around upstairs and downstairs, opening drawers and cupboards. Well, I'm not going to let them enjoy this lot, he thought, and began an orgy of destruction. He had enough sense to make no noise with breaking big items of furniture, but silently destroyed everything he could lay hands on. Clothes, sheets, towels were all ripped up. Lotions, powders, creams and food were liberally spread over carpets and furniture. Satisfied with the mess he had made, he thought, Lovely, that will give them something to think about when they get in. He made himself a drink of tea from provisions in the kitchen. But even in his enjoyment, the visions of his sister and the policeman disturbed his mind, telling him that this was the end and that he would be back inside before the day was out.

'You have nowhere to go, Harry, no one wants you, you have nothing left. You'll be locked up for ever and ever, all alone,' said the policeman, staring at him with cold eyes and blank face. He could not see a nose or mouth, only the eyes.

Can't stand this, I'll never be free of them. A terrible sense of loneliness overwhelmed him. I have nothing and no one. No future. Nobody cares if I live or die. He cursed his mother for leaving him.

'Don't worry no more, son, Mum's here,' he heard her say. He stood stock still. Die, that's the idea. If I'm dead, they can't lock me away, can they? If I went back there it would be worse than before. But I won't make it easy for them. Let's see what I can find to make a proper job of it.

He looked around him. Gas cooker, yes, that's the way. He looked through the kitchen drawers until he found a knife that was sharp but small. Lovely, and it's got a nice point an' all. Then he went to the bathroom and there in the mess he had made he found the aspirin. Not that many, but they'll have to do. Pity I got rid of all the disinfectant on the floor, I could have used that too.

Harry made himself some more tea, and with it he swallowed all the aspirin, twenty-five in all, he counted. Not really enough but they'll make me drowsy. I'm so weary. I just want to sleep and sleep. Well, I'm going for the long sleep but not until I've added to the mess here.

Harry brought a pillow down from upstairs and laid it in front of the gas oven. He turned on the oven tap and moved the pillow on to the oven floor. Taking the knife, he deliberately cut long slits in both his ankles and his wrists, delighted as the blood flowed. Lovely colour it is, best colour of all. Lying down now, he continued to cut himself wherever he could reach, and it seemed to him he was surrounded by red. He felt he was on the sea, rising and dipping with the waves. As his mind succumbed to the effect of the tablets and the loss of blood, his eyelids became too heavy to open. Just before sleep overcame him, he thought, What am I doing? I don't want this, why should I die? But it was now too late to reverse what he had started.

Part Three

Chapter Twenty-Two

1971–1991

Chief Inspector Barbrum sat at his desk looking at the old books and reports laid out before him. He had been to see the chief superintendent and told him of the deputation of six people, all telling this queer story of a haunted house. The chief had looked at him as if he'd lost his marbles, but listened to the taped recordings of the seances in grim silence.

'If that lot are wasting our time, I'll throw the book at them. God knows we have too much on our files already, but in those tapes we have a description of a murder. The thing is, where did he, whoever *he* is, leave the body? If it is all true, the body could still be lying where he left it. There won't be anything left now, though, except bones. Better get cracking, Neil. Gather all information you can from other forces on any unidentified bodies found in 1964. Better still, go and see this Monica Preston, and find out more about her sister-in-law and the children. Find out what the score is on her.'

Neil sat wondering who he could send, in circumstances such as these. He finally decided that himself and Sergeant Howe would be best. Howe could be very close-mouthed, and these people had asked him not to let the press in on any enquiry. He'd do his best on that, but knew they would sniff at the case like a dog with a bone. In the end they'd all be hammering away for a story. Still, he'd keep it quiet for as long as he could.

He called Detective Sergeant Howe into his office and told him the whole story. Howe and he had been working together for a long time. He would never reach higher grade than sergeant, but Neil knew that he was thorough. A plodder really, but in his own slow way he got more done than many of the go-getters amongst the detectives. He took time and patience to reason everything through, worked out his strategy carefully, and then ploughed straight in.

'It's a rum story you're telling me, and the tapes you've just played would do justice to a Victorian melodrama, guv. Don't like the bit about the murder though, that sounds nasty.'

'Tell you something else too you may have forgotten. Cast your mind back, Ted, fifteen years. I'd only just been promoted to inspector. We had a spate of women, especially prostitutes, being attacked. The press had a field day because we weren't coming up with any suspects, remember? You were a young copper then and I recall you were violently sick on one occasion at the mess one girl was in when we saw her.'

'By God, yes, I do remember that. We finally got a picture of the suspect and this man's sister came in and said it looked like her brother. I thought it funny at the time because she seemed so pleased with herself.' Howe scratched his head. 'Can't remember the name but it will come.'

'Shall I tell you then? Monica Carpenter, and it was her brother who stabbed himself trying to get away. You put the handcuffs on him. Now does it ring bells with you?'

'Good God, you're right. Think this Monica Preston could be Monica Carpenter then? Blimey, guv, that's a turn-up for the book. Right nasty piece of work he was, so was she in a different way. Hated her brother, she did. Watched her in the court when he was sentenced. She had a smile on her face so wide I thought it would split in two.'

'That's right, Ted. Now we two have to go and see her. Seems she's anxious to find this boyfriend of Carpenter's wife. Looking after his kid, she is, and reckons she ought to be paid for doing so. These people who came in want it kept from the press, so we have to keep quiet about the whole thing. They'll get the story though, they always do. You've read the statements and they reckon it could make things worse if there's crowds around. If, and I say if, he's the ghost, I reckon he could be nasty. We had trouble with him when we arrested him. Don't know how it was he got away, but he did. I remember the to-do when he went missing. In this book here is the report on a suicide at the address the Gordons gave, and the date agrees with the tape. Must admit I'm a bit flummoxed on this. Never had anything like it before. Still, it will be something to clear up before I retire. Like to finish it off before I go.'

Neil Barbrum and Ted Howe had been to see Monica Preston. 'A sharp-witted, sharp-tongued and garrulous woman on the look out for the best opportunity to help herself' was their assessment of her. No, she couldn't tell them anything about Charlie Lambert, had never met him. She'd just been landed with the kids to look after, that's all. Still, if he could be found she'd be glad, he ought to be paying something towards the upkeep of his own kid, oughtn't he? The best person to talk to was her nephew Mark, but they couldn't see him until the evening because he was at work, so was the girl. Well, somebody had to bring the money in, didn't they? After all, it was their brother she'd got, and until Charlie Lambert was found, they had to help.

So they asked that Mark and Samantha Lambert phone to make arrangements to see them at their convenience.

'God help everyone if the press get a whiff of this, that one would sell her soul for money. Bet she's got a bit stashed away on the quiet,' Ted Howe said as they drove away from the house.

'You're right, and she'll also pester the Gordons too, you wait and see. Still, if she gets involved in these seances she might get more than she bargained for. Be it on her own head.' Neil puffed away on his pipe. 'You know, Ted, we'll have to go to one of these psychic sittings, if they'll let us, of course. Have to see the Gordons about that. I'll ring when we get back to the office.'

Back at his office, Neil ploughed through a stack of paperwork. Never ends, he thought. I get more and more each day. He'd spent the afternoon seeing various members of his staff for their reports, advising and commenting where necessary. Good crowd really. Suppose I'm lucky with my men, they usually get results. They were hard men though, but they had seen enough in the course of their duties to make them that way. Hard they might be, but he knew how compassionate they could be to bereaved parents, or victims of crime. They all worked long hours, and for some it had caused the breakdown of their own marriages. It was true that old saying, 'If you can't stand the heat, stay out of the kitchen'. He sat thinking of the good men who had given up the job because it was either the job or their marriage. Must be getting maudlin in my old age.

The phone rang and he was surprised as he picked up the receiver to find it was seven o'clock. It wasn't unusual to work late into the night, and he didn't have a wife to think of, she had died a couple of years back with cancer. That had been a relief, better than seeing her suffer, but he missed her just as much now as when it had happened.

On the telephone was Mark Lambert. Deep voice, quiet-speaking fellow, he thought, as he arranged for them to meet. Yes, it was all right to bring his sister Samantha, good idea. 'Eight o'clock, that's fine. I'll be here.'

Neil cleared some more paperwork and made tracks for the canteen to get a snack. When I retire, I'm going to find me a quiet place where I can potter in my garden. I'll grow my own vegetables, be better than what you buy, fresher. Yes, he would like that. Have to start looking for a place soon though, his retirement day was not far off. End of the year I'll be saying goodbye to this lot. Wonder who will get my job? Good luck to him, reckon things are going to get worse, not better.

Chapter Twenty-Three

At eight o'clock, Mark and Samantha Lambert were shown into his office. Nice-looking youngsters, he thought.

'We understand from Auntie Monica you'd like to see us, sir. I'm not sure how we can help you, and we don't really know what this is all about. Anyway, she kept on and on about Charlie, and how we ought to help find him, so we decided to come. It's not unusual for her to keep on about Charlie, keeping his kid, though why, I don't know, she gets enough from the estate and what we pay, but that's the kind of woman she is.'

He's got her summed up well, thought Neil. Money from the estate, eh? What estate?

'Sit down, both of you. It's good of you to come. Would you like some tea? Not that it's much cop, mind you.'

'Thank you, we've had our meal, but a cup of tea would be nice, wouldn't it, Mark?' Samantha said, seating herself before Neil.

A poised young woman, thought Neil. Old for her years. He judged her to be about nineteen years of age.

Mark sat down. 'How can we help you, sir? I should think we know as much about the disappearance of Charlie as you do, except for one thing.'

'Oh, and what's the one thing?' Neil picked up the telephone and ordered tea for three. 'In cups mind, none of your cracked beakers.'

Mark looked at him for a while. 'You'll probably think I'm as nutty as my father. We know who our father was. He was Harry Carpenter, convicted of grievous bodily harm, way back in 1957. A psychopath, it was said, and I can well believe it from the memories I have. It was after the report that he had escaped, that Charlie disappeared, and this is where you'll find my story nutty, Chief Inspector.'

'How's that then? Why should I think that, young man? Come in,' he called, in answer to the knock on the door. In walked a constable with their tea.

'Thank you, Officer, that's very kind of you.' Samantha smiled at the young man who entered the room with tea on a tray.

She's quite a cracker, thought Neil. Got the youngster blushing too. He thanked the constable and told him he'd let him know when it was finished.

Handing out the tea, he looked at Mark. 'I'm waiting to hear what you think is nutty, young man.'

'I can't just tell you like that, have to go back a bit first. We had an awful time when we lived with our real father. I grew up years ahead of my time because of him. Can you imagine what it's like to see your mother beaten black and blue, and be too little to do anything about it? Well, that was me. I hated my father with a terrible hatred, and still do for what he did to our mum. Sam and I had to be quiet all the time, and always in our rooms by the time he came home from work. I'd hear him raving at Mum, but we couldn't do anything except stay in our rooms, as Mum said, no matter what. Well, that's no way for kids to grow up. When I hear of cases of child cruelty, I know just what they feel like. Oh, he never hit us, just never wanted us around.'

'That doesn't surprise me, about your mum, lad, but where is this leading us?'

Mark looked at him. 'I'm coming to that if you'll bear with me. One night, the raving was worse than ever before. I heard a lot of crockery being smashed and the last time I heard my father, he was bellowing that he would be back at ten o'clock, and shrieking with laughter. He said she was to get the place cleared up or she'd get another dose, then the front door slammed. I crept downstairs, terrified that he would still be there, and I found my mother in the dining room, unconscious on the floor, covered with blood and food, the dinner she'd cooked. That memory never leaves me. Anyway, eventually Mum came round and told me to get myself and Sam dressed because we were leaving that night. We had to help her dress. She was bruised, cut and scalded. I can see her face now, like a balloon.'

Without knowing it, the tears started trickling down his cheeks, and Mark, feeling acutely embarrassed, took out his handkerchief.

'Would you like to finish this another time, son?' asked Neil.

'No, I'd rather finish what I have to say, sir. We left, and the rest is a blur, but Uncle Charlie came into our lives. Sam and I had never met him before, but he was the best thing that ever happened to us. He looked after us and Mum, and took us to his place in the Forest of Dean. Very quiet little hamlet, and that's where I'll be going as soon as I can, and Sam and Charlie, little Charlie that is.

'Anyway, to get back to the story. Mum was ill for a long time. Sam and I knew nothing then about our natural father being imprisoned, or of their divorce. All we remember is being happier than we had ever been.

'When Mum married Charlie – that was in 1960 – we were adopted by Charlie and our name was changed to his. Our mum grew into a lovely-looking woman, and I had never seen her so happy and contented, but it took all of four years for that to happen.

'After about a year they had little Charlie, and we all adored him. He's a lovely kid even now, despite having been under Auntie Monica's influence. I try to combat that as much as I can, she's got a warped outlook on life, though from what she's told me about her life I'm not surprised. She doesn't wallop Charlie now, very careful she is, but it's too late. I intend to get Charlie into my care, and that's what I'm fighting for, then we're off to the Forest of Dean to live in my house there, which was Charlie's house. That sounds muddled but it's easy to explain.'

'I feel you've a lot more to say, young man, and what I suggest is that we three go and have a meal together. You may have eaten properly today, but I haven't, so how about it?' For some reason Neil had taken a great liking to these two youngsters, and it seemed to him they had had a pretty rough deal from life, from what he'd heard so far.

Sam and Mark looked at each other in surprise. They didn't expect kindness from a senior police officer, they didn't expect anything from anybody really. Sam looked at Neil and saw that under the stern exterior of the uniform and face, there were twinkling blue eyes.

'Never had children of our own, my wife and I. Probably just as well. It's hard for a young copper's wife when she's got kids, and a husband at work all hours. Causes a lot of trouble, that does. So what say, let's go and get something decent to eat, shall we?'

Neil took them to a small quiet café, and they were given a secluded table in the corner. Sam and Mark noticed that the chief inspector was known there, and the service they received was very good. The food was plain, but tasty.

'I've been coming here for years, more so since my wife died. They've looked after me well, it's a family business. Anyway, back to your story, young Mark. Tell me while we drink our coffee. Do you mind if I smoke my pipe, young lady?'

Sam shook her head at him. 'After that meal I think you deserve it,' she said. 'Can't remember when I last enjoyed a meal so much.'

Mark sat looking at his cup. 'There's gaps to fill in, but all I'll say right now is that when our father went missing from prison, Charlie disappeared shortly after. He went for a walk one day; he did quite often, and didn't come back. But this is the bit you'll think I'm nutty about. When Charlie didn't return by nine o'clock, Mum was frantic. There was no way that he would just walk out, we were all so happy. He was over the moon having young Charlie, because his first wife couldn't have children. Anyway, Mum reported Charlie missing to our local bobby, but nothing came of that. I knew it wouldn't though. I knew he was dead. The reason being that I awoke halfway through the night that he disappeared, and there he was, standing beside my bed. This sounds like I'm nuts, but truly he was just the same as if he was really there. He just said, "Sorry, Mark, take care of your mum and everyone," and then faded away. So you see, sir, although you may think I'm crazy, I know he's dead. The problem has been trying to prove it. I told Mum and I told Sam, but the authorities would never accept that as evidence, would they?'

'No, lad, reckon they wouldn't. So now I have to tell you some things, but what I tell you must remain between us three. Definitely don't tell your aunt, that would only make for more problems.'

Neil told them all he knew, of the taped recordings, everything. When he had finished, they sat in silence. Neil thought it was time to order more coffee, and promptly did so.

'So you see, we do have evidence of a murder, committed by a now dead man, who has left the body we know not where. Bit of a problem, but I'd like to clear it all up before I retire.'

'He, Charlie, must be in the Forest of Dean somewhere. That's the only place he ever went walking, isn't it, Samantha?'

Samantha looked at Mark. 'We were so happy, Chief Inspector, and then the bubble just burst.'

Mark took up the narrative again. 'Little Charlie was three then and Samantha about fourteen, I suppose. I had just left school and was wondering what to do with my life. I wanted to go to university to study sociology, but couldn't leave Mum in the state she was in. Charlie had made sure we had no money worries, but we didn't take liberties, wouldn't have been right because he was so good to us in every way. He used to talk about his first wife, Laura, and we came to feel she was an aunt who had died. From what he told us, she must have been a lovely lady. You'll think I'm even nuttier, most people would, but I've seen her too, and Mum, since she died.' Mark delved into his pocket and brought out a letter which looked as if it had been well handled. 'When Mum died, I was given this letter by our solicitor. We were, by then, living with Aunt Monica, and the others thought it was only for a short time, but you'll understand when you read this.' He handed the letter to Neil.

The letter was dated 10th September, 1968. 'Mum had talked to me one evening and got me to agree to live with our aunt, because she was afraid the authorities would take the young ones into care if we didn't go there. She wanted me with them to keep an eye on them, and when you know my aunt more you'll understand why.'

Neil took the letter and silently read it. How much this boy has had to come to terms with in life, he thought. It's a wonder he's as stable as he is.

My very dear Son,

I ask your forgiveness, my dear Mark, for the responsibility that I am placing on your shoulders. You have had to grow up long before you should, but when you read this you will, I hope, understand my reasons for what I have to do.

Your aunt is not, perhaps, the most desirable person to entrust my beloved children to, but I can see no other way. Soon you will be a man in the eyes of the law, and then you can take control of Samantha and young Charlie. I ask you to do this until they are adults. The decision I have made was not an easy one, but it has been made to spare you all, you in particular, more suffering.

When I spoke to you about going to stay with your Aunt Monica, I was not entirely truthful with you. I could not be, my son, or you would not have left me. I told you I would be having treatment for a long time and it would not be right for Samantha or Charlie to see me during that time. The truth is, Mark, that nothing can be done for me. The cancer that I have has spread too far. I have been having pain in my head for a long time as you know, and always told you it was migraine. It was not. I could have a disfiguring operation on my face but it would only keep the cancer at bay for a short while.

Forgive me, my son, and ask Samantha to do the same, for by the time you read this I will have joined Charlie and Laura. I intend to take my life, dear Mark, because I don't want you all to remember me sick and disfigured, you and Sam saw enough of that when you were young.

Think of me alive and happy as I was with you all and Charlie. God forgive me, I pray, but I must do it my way and not give you any more bad memories.

The house is yours, and the money left in trust until each of you comes of age, then you will get what is left after paying your aunt each month, enough to keep you all. The solicitor will explain.

I love you all so very much, but I must say goodbye. We will all meet again one day in God's heaven.
Mother

Neil looked up and handed the letter back to Mark. 'So that statement made by your aunt to the Gordons was true. I'm sorry, son, you two have had your share of heartaches. You said you were trying to get control of your young brother. You're of age so what's the problem?'

'Oh, Aunt Monica's fighting it because I'll be taking him to the cottage and won't have a job. She says she will go to the authorities and get control through them. Now that Sam is twenty-one years old it will be easier for me. My aunt is not worried about young Charlie being in my care, it's the money from us all she wants to keep. With both Sam and I of age now, I don't see she's got a leg to stand on;

anyway, when I tell the authorities the truth about my aunt I can't see there should be any trouble. I hope not, anyway.'

'What is there to tell about her then? Does she treat the boy badly?' Neil asked.

'Not now, but she never wanted us at all – the money, yes, but not us.' Samantha sounded quite bitter. 'She used to shout and rave at us and smack little Charlie because he cried. He'd never been used to that, you see, and he was only a baby. Mark and I took over the care of Charlie, and as we grew older she found that Mark would tolerate none of her tantrums. She's very wary of Mark, and of course, there's me now. She's not a nice woman, but then she's never known love in her life, so one has to make allowances, I suppose.

'She told me she had changed her name to Preston from Carpenter after my real father was imprisoned. Aunt Monica doesn't like to be reminded of that, but she will happily say to us that we must have some of his madness in us. Not little Charlie, of course, he's not her brother's child.'

Mark broke in, 'She doesn't raise her hand to Charlie now, I put a stop to that some years ago. Still, we'll all be happier in the cottage, but I need to get control of Charlie, away from her grasping hands.' Mark looked down. 'I'll get it somehow.'

Neil made a sudden decision, surprising himself. 'Tell you what, when I next have a weekend off, or better still, when I travel to see the chief of police for Gloucestershire, I'll come with you to your cottage if you'll have me. I'll sum up the situation there and see what can be done. Will that help?'

'Help! With someone of your standing it will be a godsend. We seem to have guardian angels come into our lives just when we need them, consider yourself one of them.' Mark put out his hand and Neil laid his into it.

'I'll see what I can do. Between us three, I don't care much for your aunt, and I remember her from many years ago, boy. I was the inspector in charge of your dad's case all those years ago. Funny what tricks life can play, isn't it?'

Chapter Twenty-Four

Neil had spent a very busy week. He had spoken to Mr and Mrs Gordon and asked that they delay any further psychic sittings with the Bants until his investigations were more productive. It was arranged that he would call on them within the next two weeks.

Contacting the chief of the Gloucestershire police, he arranged a meeting with him and the divisional head covering the Forest of Dean. Going to be a bit tricky, that, he thought.

He got Sergeant Howe working on collating birth, marriage and death certificates for Harry and Monica Carpenter, for Glenda and Harry and their children, and also for Charles and Laura Lambert, and finally for Glenda and Charles Lambert, and their son Charles.

Also, he wanted a transcript of all evidence leading up to the trial of Harry Carpenter, plus the trial and also the prison records referring to him. Let's see what he was like in prison. The prison record told him that Harry Carpenter had settled down to be a quiet and obedient prisoner with only the occasional outburst of violence. This was put down to the beneficial effects of the drugs he was given. Little did they know what was going on in his mind. Planned this murder for years, he did. Wonder how he found out where they were living? Bet that Monica comes in on it somewhere. He also wanted the police file on the suicide of Harry Carpenter. Must see what they have to say about that.

Having got Sergeant Howe organised, he contacted Mark Lambert and told him when he would be going to Gloucester. 'Can you make it then, son?'

'Oh, I'll ask for holiday time, Chief Inspector. I've got some due. Have to leave Sam to take charge of things for a few days. You'll be able to meet Nanny Dowers, our neighbour, who cared for us so well when we first went there. She's getting on a bit now, though, but still keeps an eye on the cottage. I don't let it anymore because I take Sam and Charlie there for a weekend as often as I can. Hope you won't find it too quiet.'

'Well, lad, if I like it I might try to get a place there myself, if there's one going, that is. I'll want to get to a quiet place when I retire. Anyway, we'll see when we get there.'

The following Monday, they set off in the chief inspector's car. He wore his uniform, as he was travelling officially, but looked forward to changing into casual wear later.

'Will you stay in the car until I find out if the chief there wants to see you?'

'Of course, sir. I may be of help because I know the odd little pathways he would have taken, because we often went together. Charlie never stayed on the main paths. He liked to wander through the undergrowth until he came to a clearing. He called it communing with nature. He was a very gentle soul, you know, but you couldn't play fast and loose with him. I remember one workman trying it and he came unstuck, quite surprised I was at the time, but when you recall he had his own business, he couldn't have run that successfully if he had been soft with everyone all the time, could he?'

'No, lad, don't reckon he could.' That gave food for thought. 'Own business, eh? That's where the money comes from. Wonder how much there is left.'

They drove on in companionable silence, stopping on the way for a light meal and arriving at police headquarters in Gloucester just before two in the afternoon.

Mark sat in the car for about twenty minutes, and then a young constable came out to take him to the chief constable's office. He wondered what the outcome would be, for he understood only too well how outlandish the story would sound, especially to a highly experienced police chief.

When he entered the office, Chief Inspector Barbrum introduced him to the man behind the desk.

'This is the son of the man referred to in the tapes, sir. He has not heard the tapes, only the story from myself. Would you object if he listens with us?'

'Not if he doesn't,' was the short reply. Mark sat dumbfounded as the three tapes of the rescue sittings were played. When they were finished, he could contain himself no longer. 'That man, if he is my father, makes it sound as if he loved my mother, as if she was the one at fault. That's not true. If he loved her, how could he treat her so badly? My mother, sir, was a sweet-natured person, and if you had seen her as I saw her on the night that we left, you would know how badly she was treated. That memory is ever with me, and I was only a boy of eight. She was smothered in blood, her face black and blue, and so swollen she could hardly speak. It took a long time, four years to be exact, to recover from the effects of the treatment she'd received at my father's hands. No, I won't have her blamed, in any way.'

'Don't upset yourself, lad,' Neil said. 'Some people only see things one way, their way.'

'I know that, Chief Inspector, but I'll tell you this. The only real happiness my mother ever knew was with Charlie, and the same applies to my sister and myself. If that is my father on the tapes, I could quite believe him capable of murder. He would have murdered my mother the night we left, given the chance, and Samantha and me. We were terrified of him.'

Neil and Mark arrived at the cottage at about seven o'clock, and there, as always, was Nanny Dowers ready to greet Mark.

She took one look at him and saw that he was upset. 'What have you been doing to him? Why is he like this? He looks like he did when I first saw him.' Anger showed in her face and voice.

'It's all right, Nanny. I'm just angry, that's all.' Mark tried to calm her, but he knew it wasn't just anger he felt. The afternoon's events had taken him back to when he'd found his mother so badly hurt, and to when he had first met Charlie. He was quite sure that Charlie was somewhere in the Forest of Dean, and that that somewhere was close by.

'Nanny, let me introduce Chief Inspector Barbrum to you. Don't be angry with him. I think he may well be another guardian angel, just like Charlie was.'

'If you say so.' Nanny's feathers were still ruffled. 'Come in anyway, I've got a meal ready for you both.'

Mark gave her a hug. 'When have you *not* had a meal ready for us, Nanny? You have always looked after us.'

'Get off, you daft thing.' Nanny Dowers bustled away to make the tea. 'Go and put your things away, son, while I get your tea, then we can talk.'

Mark led Neil upstairs and showed him to a spare room. 'Charlie had the place extended soon after we came here, he said it was too small for us all. We didn't mind how small, just to feel safe was enough for us.'

Shortly after, they were sitting in the lounge drinking a welcome cup of tea.

'Well, what's all this about then?' Nanny asked. 'Must be something important for a police chief to travel this far from London.'

'It is, Nanny, it is,' Mark said. 'You remember when Charlie went missing, and we all knew he wouldn't do that willingly, didn't we?'

'We did indeed. A happier man I've never seen, so there's no way he'd have gone off just like that.'

'Well, I'll tell you how things are,' and Mark related all that he knew. Nanny's eyes widened with shock as she listened. 'So you think he's still around here then? I know he used to enjoy his walks. Used to say, "Breathes new life into me, Nanny," when he came back, only one day he didn't, did he? Such a state your mother was in. I couldn't understand when she sent you all away. I felt that she didn't trust me to look after you, but when I read the letter she left me, I understood. You'd been through too much to see any more. I'll never forget the state of her, or you and Sam, when you first came, that I won't.'

'Well, anyway, we've been given six men to help search the area for one week, so let's hope we come up with something in that time.' Neil sounded somewhat peeved. 'Doesn't give us much time, but anyway, we start tomorrow.'

'Well, that's tomorrow. Tonight you've to sit and eat the meal I've prepared, then I reckon you'd better get to bed early. I'll wash up in the morning for you.' Nanny got up to go. She still wasn't sure of the chief inspector.

'We'll wash up tonight, Mrs Dowers. I'm quite used to looking after myself since my wife died. Can't put too much on you, wouldn't be fair. See you in the morning, and thanks for cooking that lovely meal for us.'

Chapter Twenty-Five

It was Thursday before they found the remains of Charlie. Neil kept Mark by his side throughout the search. Neil had been pushing on through the undergrowth, talking to Mark while he did so. The young police officers were either side of them, searching the very dense area of growth. One stopped and called to Neil, 'Chief, I think I've found something.'

'You stay here, lad, and I'll go and take a look-see,' Neil had said, but Mark followed him. A shoe was just visible, protruding from the grasses. 'Over here, all of you,' called Neil, and was soon surrounded by the others.

They tore away at ferns and twigs and soon revealed a body, or what was left of it. From the chest a knife was sticking up at right angles, and the cloth was rotting away. All that remained was mostly a skeleton, but under the rags of cloth would be found scraps of hard, dead flesh.

'Right you, contact headquarters and let them know,' Neil said to one youngster who looked decidedly green. 'Don't touch any part of what's there, leave it to forensics.' He turned and saw Mark behind him. 'What are you doing here, son, I told you to stay where you were.'

'I wanted to see for myself. If it does prove to be Charlie, then at least we can give him a decent burial.' It seemed impossible to Mark that these grisly remains were once their dearly beloved stepfather. 'Oh Charlie, what an end, but at least we've found you now. I wonder if you knew how much we loved you.'

In his ear a voice that was Charlie's said, 'Yes, Mark, I do know. I love you too.' Mark looked around but there was no one beside him.

'What are you looking for, Mark?' Neil looked at him in surprise.

'I'll tell you later, sir, not now. It's not the right time.' Mark found that tears were streaming down his cheeks.

'You lot, stay here, and don't touch anything. I won't be far away. Come on, lad, take a walk with me.'

Neil took Mark's arm and led him away back to the pathway. 'Don't be ashamed of your tears, lad, they're natural. I cried when my wife died, couldn't help it. Doesn't mean to say you're weak, you know, only that you loved someone.'

'Why did he have to do that? He would never have got Mum back. What was the point? My God, he must have had a twisted mind.'

'As soon as the others get here we'll away to your home and have us a nice cup of tea. You'll be better there, shouldn't be long now. Just remember, you're not on your own. Don't have any kids of my own, and I've taken quite a fancy to you and your sister. I'll do what I can to make it all easier, but you'll still have a load of hassle from the press, to say the least.'

'Poor Charlie, to end like that, after all he'd done for us.' As Mark sobbed out his sorrow, the older man put his arm round his shoulder and drew Mark to him. Poor little devil, his life has surely had its bad periods. Wonder why some suffer more than others in this life? Don't suppose there's any answer to that one, and I've asked it often enough, God knows.

It was about an hour later that they were in the lounge of the cottage, drinking tea. Neil had asked Mrs Dowers to get a small bottle of brandy from the village shop, telling her to say it was an emergency but to say nothing of what had happened. He made sure Mark had a good measure and gave a drop to Nanny Dowers. He didn't need it himself, he was too used to appalling sights for it to affect him, but he did feel sad for the boy. Still, what's done is done, and can't be undone. Got to get on with the job in hand. The sooner the better.

Later that day, Neil and Mark sat before the fire in the sitting room. Nanny had cooked a meal, but Mark could eat very little. Neil saw that her fussing was grating on Mark. 'Leave him be tonight, Mrs Dowers, he'll eat better tomorrow. Had a shock today and needs time to get over it.'

'He'll be ill if he don't eat,' Nanny had protested.

'No, he won't. He'll eat tomorrow, you'll see. Feel better tomorrow he will, believe me, I know, I've seen it often. Leave the boy alone today, he's got a lot of sorting out to do in his mind.'

'Don't know about that,' Nanny snorted. 'A young man needs his food, he does.'

'Well, I'll see he gets something before we go to bed, leave it to me.'

She'd gone off in a huff and still worried. 'See that he does then. Don't want him ill.'

So now they were sitting quietly in front of the fire and Neil left Mark to his thoughts for a while. The afternoon had been a busy one, with the chief inspector for the area coming in to see them both. Tomorrow they would have to go into Gloucester to see the chief again, make written statements, and later on, attend the coroner's court.

'At least he should be able to get the estate settled properly. Think I'll ask for some time off, in case I can help. I expect the press will be pestering us soon. At least I'm here and can deal with them, or get the Gloucestershire police to do it.'

'I'm sorry, sir, I'm being rude sitting here in silence. The trouble is, I don't have anything to say.'

'Don't worry about it, son. I didn't expect you to talk your head off anyway, but you can answer a question for me if you will.'

'If I can, sir, I will,' Mark replied.

'When we were in the Forest I asked you what you were looking for. You suddenly turned as if you expected to see someone or something. Would you tell me about it?'

'Oh, you'll think I'm as mad as my father, my real father.'

'Try me, I might surprise you,' Neil said, with a twinkle in his eye.

'Well, sir, I was looking at... at what was there, and in my mind I was telling Charlie how much we'd loved him. There was a voice in my right ear, Charlie's voice, telling me he did know and he loved us too. It was so real, I expected him to be standing there. Suppose it does sound daft, but it happened.'

'It doesn't sound daft to me, son. When I lost my Madge, I'd find myself talking to her as if she was there, and although I didn't see or hear anything, I felt she was close by and answering me. Not the same as having them there with you, but a comfort just the same. No, you don't sound daft to me. I've heard a lot about people like you; natural psychics. You'll have to see about it. Don't know where to tell you to go, of course, because I've never taken an interest in that sort of thing. For all the cranks we have telling us things when there's a murder – oh, so sorry, lad, shouldn't have said that. However, the fact remains, occasionally we do have someone come up with facts not known to the public, and these people are totally unconnected with the enquiry. So you see, although I'm what you might call a hard-bitten policeman, my mind is still open to some things. That's one reason why this case interested me so much. I'm just glad the chief super let me carry on with it.'

The village was agog at all the police activity. They had never before seen so many policemen. When they heard that it could be Charlie Lambert that had been found in the Forest, they were stunned, but did wonder why a high-ranking policeman was staying in the village with Mark. When somebody asked if Mark was suspected, Mrs Dowers really showed her anger. 'That's the daftest suggestion I've ever heard in my life. Anyway the chief inspector seems to have quite taken to Mark, looking after him well, he is, so don't none of you go bothering them.'

Nanny was right, Neil was looking after Mark. He let him sleep late, then woke him with a cup of tea.

'Did you sleep at all, lad?' he asked.

'Oh yes, I have, slept like a log, much to my surprise.' Mark replied. 'I feel much better this morning, and hungry.'

'That's the ticket. Got a lot to do today, son, so when you've had your tea come down for your breakfast. I'm doing bacon and eggs that I've found in the fridge. I'm a bit peckish myself.'

Having seen Nanny Dowers to assure her that Mark was all right, they made their way into Gloucester to police headquarters. 'Better to get things done as quick as we can. Have to come back for the inquest, though,' Neil said.

'After that I might start looking for a place near here. Must say I like the peace and quiet. We've got to get little Charlie away from that grasping aunt of yours, sooner the better too. Think I'll take some leave and help you sort things out, that's if you want me to, of course.'

'I'd be very grateful for any help, sir, but I don't want to interfere in your life,' Mark replied.

'Nothing much in my life since my wife went. I think I'll adopt you all as the children I never had, not legally of course. Still, anyone who tries to pull a fast one on you will have me to contend with first. Reckon you need help and someone behind you that your aunt won't play fast and loose with. Oh, I remember her from way back.'

They spent most of the day at police headquarters writing out statements, and Mark answering what seemed to him endless questions. Neil telephoned his chief and told him what had happened and that he would be back tomorrow. The inquest was set for Friday of the next week to allow the forensic staff to collate their findings.

They arrived back at the cottage to be met by a crowd of pressmen. Questions were shouted from all directions.

'You go in, boy. Leave this to me,' Neil said. Turning to the press, he told them they would get more information from the local police. He couldn't tell them any more than that a body had been found. 'Don't know who it is until the investigations are completed.'

'How is it you came here looking for a body, Chief?' one asked.

'From information received,' was the short reply. 'Can't say more now, you'll have to wait for the inquest. Goodnight, lads. Nothing more to say. Don't bother coming again.'

With that he shut the door on them. They didn't get much more from the villagers either. 'Close-mouthed lot,' was the general opinion.

Chapter Twenty-Six

Neil had reported to his chief early on the morning of his return.

'I'll go to see the Gordons and probably join in their next seance, see what goes on, that's if they'll let me. Think we'd better do a check on all six of them, though; from what I saw of the Bant couple, they'd have been kids at the time of the murder, if it was committed in 1964. Still, as we know, that doesn't rule them out, does it?'

'Well, I suppose I'll get first-hand information on it if you do go. Better keep it close to your chest, though. We don't want the police force made a laughing stock. What I'm interested in, is if Harry Carpenter was away all those years, and his place was let, how did he get the chance to get in and gas himself? Look into it, Neil.'

'I've got Howe working on that one. That has puzzled me too, also how Carpenter knew where to find Lambert. If the place wasn't let at the time, you'd think the gas wouldn't be on? Could have just been off at the mains, though, between lets. Anyway, better go and sort out the pile of papers on my desk. Lots of backlog there, I know.'

'Report to me when you have more to go on. I await the inquest with interest.'

Neil went back to his office and began to plough through the work before him. Later in the morning he telephoned Mrs Gordon and requested a meeting with the six people who had come to his office to report a murder. 'When we've discussed it, we'll take it from there. I'd like to be present at the next sitting and I might bring along the son of the man in the tape to see you, if he wants to come.' It was left that Mrs Gordon would telephone him to tell him when they could all meet for discussion.

Later that evening, Neil rang Mark and asked if they could meet for a chat, and at nine o'clock they were sitting in the corner of the lounge bar at a nearby public house.

'How did the family take the news of finding the body that we think is Charlie Lambert?' Neil asked.

'Sam and young Charlie were very upset, but Sam wasn't surprised. She knew, like I did, that Charlie would not have just upped and left us. Aunt Monica can only think of the money she can't get out of him for young Charlie, and has kept on and on to me that I must provide for him. I've made it clear that I intend to take Charlie away. I'm not in her good books. All I get is "After all I've done for you" and in a way I suppose she's right.'

'I knew you'd have trouble with her. You haven't mentioned tapes or anything, have you?'

'No, I haven't, but she's demanding to know why the police keep wanting me. Says that won't go down well with the authorities. She's right, but I can't say why you want to talk to me, can I?' Mark was looking puzzled.

'Well, lad, it's like this. I'm going round to see Mr and Mrs Gordon and the others, and I wondered if you'd like to come along?'

'Not if I have to see them in that house. Too many bad memories.'

'We won't be going back to where you lived, but next door. We'll be meeting the people involved in the tape, including the medium, I hope. I want to be in on the next sitting they have. Want to see what happens.'

'I don't know if I want to be that involved.' Mark looked alarmed. 'Don't know if I could take that, not so soon after finding Charlie.'

'Well, don't worry about it, son. I'll let you know when I can see them and you can decide then. No panic about it.'

They spent the rest of the evening talking of other things. As they said goodnight, Neil said, 'If I were you, son, I'd go to your solicitor without delay and see about your rights over young Charlie. Your aunt could tie you in knots, you know. Remember, I'm here if you need me. In any case, we'll travel together on Thursday evening for the inquest on Friday, if that's all right, and I might beg for a bed for the night.'

Mark seemed pleased that he would have company, for he wasn't looking forward to the inquest at all.

The coroner's court was full for the inquest. Mark was surprised at the number of village people present. The dental evidence proved that the body found had been that of Charles Lambert, and forensic evidence stated that death had occurred from stab wounds. Date of death, inconclusive, but had occurred approximately seven years previously. The verdict was – 'Killed by person or persons unknown' and a death certificate was duly issued to that effect.

A number of the villagers came up to Mark to express their sadness that so nice a man had met with such a violent end, and hoped that the killer would eventually be found. All Mark could do was to thank them. As the pressmen started badgering him for a statement, Neil took over.

'He's had a hard time, lads. I'd say he was shocked, wouldn't you? Let's leave it at that. It's very hard for relatives when this sort of thing happens.'

'Oh,' one journalist said, 'but he was only the adopted son, wasn't he?' which brought an immediate response from Mark. 'He may not have been my real father by blood, but he was a real father to me because of the love he gave. Don't rate him as second-hand because he was my stepfather. He was adored by all the family, and I don't wish to say any more.'

'Leave him alone,' one of the villagers said. 'We knew Charlie, he was a lovely man. Go and write your sensational bits. Just leave the boy alone.'

'That's enough,' Neil said. 'No more to say, lads, you might as well go, you can see you're not welcome.'

'Only doing our job,' came the reply, with nods and shouts of agreement all round.

'I know that, boys, but there isn't any more to say, is there? Charlie Lambert was a very nice man, liked by all, respected by the villagers, and much loved by his family. We all feel sad about how he died; now what else can I say? I think you'll find everyone agrees.'

'Yes, we do,' the villagers shouted. 'Now leave us all alone, go back to your papers, or whatever. We'll keep our sorrow to ourselves.'

Neil got Mark into his car. He had attended the inquest in his official capacity, so he was in uniform.

'How come the police are so protective towards the family, then?' one pressman shouted. 'They don't usually bother that much.'

'Then all I can say is, you don't know a policeman when you see one. We don't always wear uniform, you know, but we do try to support families who are in sorrow, like this.'

With that, Neil shut the car door. With loud cheers from the villagers ringing in their ears, they drove away.

'Thank you, Chief Inspector. I must say I'm a bit surprised at all the help you've given. After all, you must have lots of other things to do. Still, I'm very grateful. I would have found it very hard coping on my own.'

'You're not on your own, lad. Don't have any children of my own, so I've sort of adopted you and your brother and sister. Someone has to help you sort out that grasping aunt of yours. Would you like me to come to a solicitor with you? Have you seen one yet?'

'No, I haven't.' Mark sat slumped in the seat. 'Couldn't see much point until the death was official. I don't know of a good solicitor, anyway.'

'Ah well, I'll make arrangements with mine. I'll ask George to my home one evening and you and your sister and brother can meet him and get it all sorted out with him. I'll let you know when. Do me good to do a bit of cooking. Don't bother much for myself, being on my own, so it will be nice to have company. I'll come and pick you up. Best not to tell your aunt or the others that you'll be seeing a solicitor though, might cause more problems. Get the facts straight first, that's the best idea. What do you say?'

'Well, I told Nanny Dowers you might be another guardian angel like Charlie, and seems like you are. I would be grateful for help, I must admit.' Mark was surprised at how fast things were moving, and as they drove back to the cottage Mark heard in his right ear, 'This man will look after you, make sure you look after him when he needs it.' And the voice was Charlie's.

Chapter Twenty-Seven

The inquest had been held two weeks ago, and Neil was driving to pick up Mark, who had agreed to meet Mr and Mrs Gordon and the others.

'I wonder how much I'll remember of the road when we go there,' Mark mused. 'I haven't been back, ever, I couldn't face it.'

'Well, I'm glad you're coming, son. Sergeant Howe, my assistant, has done a lot of work on this case, and I'd like to introduce you to him. We'll meet him there. He's going in his own car. Thought it best to have the two of us in it all. Two police reports are better than one, where it is a tricky situation.'

'Yes, I suppose they would be,' Mark replied, but he wondered what he was letting himself in for.

Later, when they were all gathered and introductions had been made, Neil told the six people who had first come in with the tapes that he had investigated their backgrounds to clear them of any implication in the murder. This caused some understandable hostility.

'Well, you see, it had to be done, and I'm happy you are all in the clear. We know where each one of you was on the alleged date, and certainly for a period of two years before as well as after. It's not every day we get told of a murder in the way you told us, and for all we know, one of you could have been pulling a fast one. Very serious business it is to waste police time, too precious to be wasted.'

'I bet we were the first to be investigated,' Mr Bant said. 'We are considered to be cranks by most people. It's understandable, I suppose. What you don't understand, you are afraid of.'

'You are right there,' Neil replied. 'I don't understand any of it, neither does Sergeant Howe, but we are trying.'

'We don't understand it either.' Jack Gordon's outrage was still evident. 'As far as I am concerned, I'd rather sell up and be done with it.'

'But then it will never be cleared up,' Laura Gordon said. 'How can we leave things as they are? Besides, it's our home, and I want to live there.'

'Have you changed it at all?' Mark asked. 'I don't much care for going in there. On the tape, he, my father I suppose, makes it sound like my mother was a gold-digger and a no good woman. It wasn't like that at all. Her life was hell on Earth, and so was my sister's and mine. We were too scared to move or speak, he was so violent.'

'I'm glad you've come,' Mrs Bant broke in. 'It gives us a better idea of the whole issue and how to deal with it. We want to have another sitting in there, but going on the past record, it could be violent. Still, we did warn you, Inspector.'

'You did that, and you also said that we mustn't come in uniform. Just additional people that's all we'd be. Sergeant Howe wants to come too, and it's better to have two police reports. My chief won't think I'm going nutty, no offence, before I retire.'

'What about you, Mark?' Mrs Bant asked. 'I know Mrs Gordon has some psychic ability, and you have an abundance. I can see so many protectors around you, and others, your mother, she tells me, and another woman, but no relation, and a man, Charlie, he says.'

'I'm glad you see Charlie and Mum, and Aunt Laura, as we came to call her. Charlie talked a lot about her, his first wife. I thought I was queer in the head, because I've seen them all. I saw him in the night on the day he disappeared. I wasn't frightened, well you couldn't be of Charlie, but I was puzzled. I've heard him too, speaking to me, but I thought it was my imagination.'

'No, Mark, not your imagination. You are a natural medium, but you do need to be trained to use the psychic ability properly,' Mr Bant said. 'That can take years.'

'Oh, I'm not sure I want to do that,' said Mark, looking worried.

'Well, you would have to think carefully before you decide yes or no,' was the reply.

Neil broke in. 'Isn't this taking us away from why we are here? I want to be present at the next seance or whatever you call it. We'll bring our own tape recorder, and a camera if possible, then there can be no question of a recording that's been tampered with, can there?'

'You are right,' Mr Bant said. 'We have to decide who will be present. We don't want too many people, that will only make matters worse.'

Two weeks later, Mark found himself sitting with a group of people in a house he had vowed never to enter again. He had had a long discussion with Mr and Mrs Bant and Mrs Gordon. Although full of apprehension he had been assured by Mrs Bant that he had so many protectors in spirit that nothing could harm him, and the same applied to Mrs Gordon. Their protectors would encircle all those at the sitting to keep them safe. The sitting, however, was likely to be violent, and very upsetting for Mark, and he must be very sure before agreeing to attend. He would probably be reminded of many things he had tried so hard to put at the back of his mind, but then to put these bad memories into the right perspective, things had to be faced and dealt with. He must always remember that God loved him, and had work for him to do, and the past which was so painful to remember had been tests to prepare him for the work God wanted him to do in his future life.

So, with his mind full of mixed thoughts, which were continually going round in circles, he sat there wondering what was to happen.

Neil and Sergeant Howe sat on either side of him. On a cabinet by the door was a small movie camera and extra lights had been put on, as it was hoped to film as well as tape what occurred. As Neil explained, police chiefs were sceptical about alleged psychic phenomena, and if they, as policemen, could capture the happenings on film and taped recordings, with all equipment having been sealed in the laboratory, there couldn't be any argument about it. Neither he nor Sergeant Howe knew what to expect and sat there hoping they were not being made fools of.

With them were Mr and Mrs Bant sitting further down the room, and on either side of them were Laura Gordon and Fay Oliver. Their husbands were sitting beside them, so there were nine people in all.

So as not to draw attention to the house, they had entered quietly through the back door, and as their numbers had increased, their chairs were close to the walls.

Fortunately, Mark had been able to evade all questions directed at him by Aunt Monica, who was unable to contain her curiosity as to why the police constantly wished to talk to him. 'Hope you've not been up to no good like your mad father,' she had said, and this had started Mark wondering about his future and marriage if he ever met the right girl. He wasn't at all sure about having children, although he would love them dearly, but could such a mental state be hereditary?

It just shows how one person can destroy others' lives, he thought. Suppose I did have children, and one turned out to be like my real father? It would be too much to hope that they would be like Dad Charlie.

Poor Sam was going through the same uncertainty. She was considering entering nursing, but with the family background she didn't think she would have much chance of being accepted. Mark had told her about tonight and he knew she was not keen on his being involved.

When this was over, he and Sam were to have their evening with Neil, and Mark would discuss his problems with Neil's solicitor, but, as Neil said, 'One step at a time, boy. Let's clear this up and go from there.'

The vicar had not been able to attend, the strain was too much, and he was still suffering from the effects of previous sittings. What he had heard and witnessed was beyond his understanding, for he had never had to cope with anything like it before in all his years in the Church. He had decided that all of it was to do with the devil's work. Mark didn't blame him, for he was also full of doubt.

Chapter Twenty-Eight

When Mr Bant spoke, it made Mark jump, so engrossed was he in his thoughts.

'If you've got your camera set and filming, and your tape recorder working, I suggest we begin,' he said to Neil.

'We're ready,' was Neil's short reply.

Mr Bant continued, 'Whatever happens, you must all remain in your chairs or places. Do not, I repeat do not, break the circle of people. I will lead the way. Now, first we will pray, and throughout the sitting I want you to send out your thoughts to help the disturbed soul who is troubling this house. We hope tonight we will be able to clear the past away so that Mr and Mrs Gordon can live here in peace. We have been instructed by our guides in what to do. You must all understand that you must stay in your places until I tell you that you may move. Now, let us begin. Let us pray.

'Divine and Infinite Father God, Creator of all things, we ask for your love to surround us all, that the wings of our guardian angels go around us to protect us at all times.

'We ask, Father, for those on high in spirit to help us in our task to release the earthbound soul in this house, that they will be able to take him to a place of safety, peace and love, so that his tortured mind can be at rest. We know, Father, you love your creation and we come to you for help, we knock, and you open the door to us, we ask, and we will receive. Let us be as one with you this night, to bring peace, harmony and love into this house. We place ourselves in your protective care, and ask that our guides may be helped by our love to do their work. Amen.'

Mark looked at Mrs Bant and saw that she was asleep, but he felt worried by the way she was breathing so deeply. Eventually her breathing quickened, and her head, which had slumped forward, lifted.

'Good evening, God bless you,' said a voice.

Mr Bant replied, 'God bless you.'

The discarnate voice then continued. 'We have much to do this night to help the soul who is trapped here. My friends will shortly bring him before us. Mark, my son, do not be afraid, no harm will come to you, or any here tonight. What you see and hear will distress you, but, I hope, also lift you. If any of you feel hands upon you, do not feel afraid, they are your loved ones helping us.'

Mark felt a hand on his shoulder, and someone kissed his cheek.

'My son, I love you,' he heard, and it was his mother's voice. He turned his head to the right and heard his mother say, 'Charlie and Aunt Laura are here with you also, don't be afraid, we will let no harm come to you.'

Neil sat there stunned. He had heard every word. He looked over to Sergeant Howe and saw a look of astonishment on his face. Well, it can't just be me, he thought.

The discarnate voice spoke again through Mrs Bant. 'No, Neil, it is not just you who heard. You too have a loved one standing behind you. Madge, your wife. You all have loved ones here. You, Sergeant Howe, you have a tall man, very well-built, behind you. He is anxious for me to tell you he is here. He is proud of you, he wants you to know that. He has a policeman's uniform on and he holds a truncheon in his hand. He says he had to use it in his day when things got rough down at the docks. He says he passed to spirit suddenly of a heart condition. It took him a while to understand what had happened. He says policemen are doubting Thomases – just like you. Now you will understand that to pass to spirit is like passing from one room to another. Do not look so shocked. He has much love for you, your mother and all the family. He will meet your mother when her time comes.'

Mark looked at Sergeant Howe. His face was a picture – mouth open, eyes wide. Looking around at the others, Mark saw Mrs Gordon smiling, but Mr Gordon looked as if he had been fixed in one position.

The discarnate voice spoke again, and there was much compassion in the voice.

'Mr Gordon, relax, you are not alone. Your mother is with you. She tells me she was killed by a bomb in the war, a direct hit on the house. A sister and brother were lost also. They are here tonight, your mother's name was Hilda, your sister was called May, and your brother was Arthur. Such handsome children; your brother says he was with you on D-Day. He says he pushed you away from the shell that fell near you. Do you remember it? You thought you must have tripped. No, it was Arthur keeping you as safe as he could.'

'I don't believe it,' Mr Gordon said. 'How can you know all these things?'

'I know because they tell me. They have always looked after you. You should have listened to Laura. You will not laugh at her in future, you will have learned a lesson, your mother says.'

'Wish I'd listened, then we wouldn't be here now,' Mr Gordon exploded.

'The house and its occupant needed your wife to help the sad conditions here. Homes should be happy havens of peace and love, but this house has suffered. Tonight we hope to complete our work, not as we would have wished, but the only way possible.'

Mark listened to the exchange of words, and although he felt shy he had to ask, 'Why do you need all of us here, why couldn't you do it on your own?'

'Because, my son, the disturbed soul in this house cannot be reasoned with. We need you all here to help build up the psychic power. You are a very strong psychic but need to have it channelled correctly, and Mrs Gordon is the same. The others of you who so kindly came have a degree of psychic power, but are not strong individually. However, together it makes the power strong.

'You are wondering, Mr and Mrs Oliver, why you are left out of things. You also have a loved one, a little girl, who tells me her name is June. She was born in June, that is why you named her so. She passed when she was eight years old after a road accident, and you thought you had lost her for good, but no, she is often with you. Have you sometimes wondered why things are in a different place to where you left them?'

'Yes,' said Fay. 'I thought I was being absentminded.'

'No, it was June trying to show you she was there. She says, "I love you Mummy and Daddy. I'm not in that earth where they laid me. I have lots of playmates, and we have a lovely time. Do not cry for me, I am happy".'

'My God,' said John Oliver. 'My little girl. I thought we'd lost her for good. My God.'

'Now, my friends, we must get down to work.' While the others were talking, Mark had been aware of the sound of many footsteps in the rooms above. It seemed people were walking from room to room, back and fro, and he heard the murmur of voices, with an occasional voice raised as if annoyed. He didn't know if anyone else had heard, but he assumed that they had.

As the room fell silent, there was a roar from above.

'What the hell do you think you are doing, what are you playing at?'

There was the sound of a struggle and much cursing upstairs. Mark was shocked. That was his father's voice, a voice he would never forget. It was like going back years to when he was a little boy. Mark pulled his attention back as the discarnate voice spoke again.

'My friends will shortly bring the disturbed earthbound one here, but they have to prepare him first, so that you cannot be harmed. It is not easy for your mother, Mark. She has not been here since she left all those years ago, and has not seen your father in all that time. Do not worry, the protectors for you all are here. You will understand my meaning later.'

As he finished speaking, there was the sound of many feet coming slowly downstairs. An angry voice bellowed, 'Get your hands off me, who do you think you are? Get out of my house, nobody asked you to come.'

The door flew open and a cold blast swept into the centre of the room. Someone stumbled and the floorboards shook as if a person had fallen.

'Hey, watch it, bloody fools.' This was followed by sniggering and the voice sang, 'Ring a ring o' roses, a pocket full of posies, atishoo, atishoo, all fall down.' Another burst of laughter, raucous and shrieking. 'That's what happened to those daft women I dealt with, they all fell down, made sure of that. Gave 'em a good kicking too, just for good measure. Nobody wanted to go with them when I'd finished, they looked bloody terrible.' This was followed by a very loud burst of maniacal laughter. Gradually it quietened down.

'What are you lot doing here? Who gave you permission to come to my house, I didn't, clear off. Get this thing off me, I'll soon kick you out just like I have everyone else.'

The discarnate voice spoke, 'My son, you have to come with us. You cannot stay any longer.'

'What do you mean, this is my house, I can stay as long as I want. What are you having here, a party? Painted up like a lot of bloody savages, clear off.'

Mark found himself back in time. The voice was indeed his father's, the shouting and the laughter brought back the long-forgotten tension within him. He felt his mother's hand tighten on his shoulder.

'Be still, my son.'

'Glenda, you bitch, you decided to come back then, you crawled back here. I suppose you want me to take you in again, that's a joke, dirty slut.'

'Harry, look at the young man in front of Glenda, do you know him?' It was the voice of the discarnate one.

'''Course I don't know him, why should I? Face is familiar though.'

'It is your son, Harry, grown to manhood.'

'Don't be bloody daft, my son's just a kid. Kids! Nothing but a squalling nuisance. I'd have shoved them in the river if I'd had my way, just like I did that man. I got out of that place by hiding in the rubbish. Then I saw this old man on his bike so I pushed him off and bashed him unconscious. I pinched all his clothes and shoved him in the water. It was lovely watching all the bubbles as he went down. Smashing that was. My daft sister wrote to tell me where my Glenda and her fancy man lived. Gloating she was. I'd take the smirk off her face if she was here. But you, Glenda, you dirty bitch, I'll deal with you as I dealt with the others. They won't ply their trade again and neither will you.'

'Leave my mother alone,' Mark said. 'You can't hurt her now.'

'Help me off this floor, you lot, I'll soon show you what I can do. Bloody little sod, talking to me like that.'

Mark could clearly see his father and many more spirit people also. It seemed quite natural to him.

'You are nothing but a small man trying to be a big man. I used to hate you with a terrible hate, and longed for the day when I was grown up enough to beat you as you beat my mother, but I no longer hate you, I pity you. If those poor women looked anything like my mother did on the night we left, then it's a wonder they lived.'

'Oh, they lived, I saw them. One had a flattened nose; lovely to see, and that one in a wheelchair, ha, great. They won't be wanted by any man now.' Harry shrieked with laughter. 'Did them proper, I did.'

'You did that all right,' Neil said.

'Mind your own business, you. 'Ere, I've seen you before, and you,' looking at Sergeant Howe and then at Neil. 'Just get out of here, all of you, I've had enough.'

Neil was tempted to say he'd come for him again but realised it would make matters worse if he did.

Mark could clearly see his father struggling to get up off the floor. His legs were kicking around in circles, but his arms were secured in a straitjacket. Laura cried out as Harry's foot struck her leg, and her husband felt his chair rock as he turned to help her. It was with some difficulty that he kept himself and his chair upright.

Mark watched his father getting more and more frantic in his struggles, twisting and turning and becoming more and more angry. 'Bastards, I'll kill you, get out of my house. Sodding bastards, what do you think you're all gaping at, get out, out.' Harry was beside himself with rage.

Fay fell to the floor, banging her head as she fell, and as her husband went to help her, he too fell, shouting with pain as Harry's legs kicked him where he lay.

'You bugger, I'll get you, let me get up and you'll see,' Harry screamed in anger. As he twisted nearer to him, Mark saw the spirit protectors, Red Indians and black warriors, stiffen. There were twanging and thudding sounds many times over.

'What are you doing, bloody savages, you nearly hit me, playing with your bows and arrows. Think you're having fun, do you? Go on, laugh, or are you afraid to, think you'll crack your paint, sodding lot of savages.'

As Harry drew near to him with murder showing in his face, Mark saw the spears held by the men in front of him go down to the floor, and more arrows thudded to the floor around his father. The spears surrounded Harry, and as he moved so the spears moved closer.

The discarnate voice spoke again.

'My son, you cannot move. You are surrounded and might as well surrender.'

'Like hell I will, bloody savages. Who do they think they are, coming in to my house and taking over?'

'My son, you have to go where they take you. Your heart burns with anger against life and all around you. Go, my son, soon you will feel at peace. You cannot stay here, they will not let you. Every move you make here will be stopped. Come, let us take you where you will be safe.'

'You mean, where they can't get at me? They won't be able to get at me?'

'No, my son, go with my friends and find peace. Go now.'

Mark saw his father weeping, his face full of fear. At the slightest move towards him or anyone else in the room, the arrows thudded down and the spears grew closer.

'You're right, it's not safe here anymore,' he heard his father say. 'By God, it's not. Let's get out of here, the place has been taken over by savages, it's not safe here anymore, bloody squatters. I want to go away, they frighten me. Don't let them get me, wait for me, wait for me.' Harry's voice grew fainter and fainter until it could no longer be heard.

The discarnate voice spoke once more.

'Be at peace, my friends, all is well. You will not be troubled again. My little one will wake soon, take care of her. God bless you all.'

Mrs Bant's head slumped to her chest and she remained inert. Mark saw a white-robed figure leave her body and fade away, and he could no longer see any other spirit people. He heard, 'Remember we love you, my son,' and felt his mother's hand leave his shoulder.

He looked around the room and felt he was waking from a sleep.

Mr Bant spoke. 'Let us pray together and give thanks.' He was standing behind his wife, supporting her with his hands.

'Dear Father God, we thank you for the love and help we have received this night. We thank you, Father, for your wondrous works. We thank you for the help and protection from your world of spirit. We ask that your light shine upon us all, now and always, and we ask that peace, love and harmony enter this house and remain evermore. Amen.'

Mrs Bant sighed and moved, and her husband held her while she awoke. She looked around her but did not speak.

'It's all right, dear, you're safe. Our work is done. When you feel able, we will go to our friends next door and rest awhile.' He looked around the room. 'I hope no one is hurt,' he said.

Fay and John Oliver stood up, saying they felt a bit bruised. Jack Gordon still looked stunned, his wife was still rubbing her leg but she was smiling. There was a cut on Fay's forehead where she had struck a chair when she fell, and her husband was rubbing his hip and limping.

'The atmosphere is so different here now. There's a friendly feeling, not like before.'

Mr Bant said, 'No, not like before, you will be all right now. Chief Inspector, you'd better gather up your camera and recorder, ready to go. Our work here is now finished.'

Chapter Twenty-Nine

They all sat in Fay and John's sitting room, drinking a welcome cup of tea. Laura had made sandwiches earlier and was handing them round. Neil was hungry. Sergeant Howe was still bemused.

'How could they have known about my dad, and Mum won't be long before she joins him, she has cancer.'

'You didn't tell me that, Ted,' Neil said. 'It must be a worrying time for you.'

'No, Chief, I didn't say anything because you have been through the mill yourself. It's nice to think we shall all meet again some day though. She's been a good old mum to me and the family. We thought she'd go to pieces when Dad died, but she seemed to end up giving us strength instead. She's always said she'd be with him again one day. Strong churchgoers they were.'

Mr Bant smiled. 'Well, Sergeant, your father's message will not be any surprise to her, will it? What did you see, Mark? I watched you and your eyes were everywhere. You saw all that happened, didn't you?'

'Yes, I did,' Mark replied. 'But I still can't say how I feel. When it was over, it was like awakening from a dream. I do know I lost all the fear and anger I'd felt for my father for so long. What a poor soul to be so angry all the time. His mind must have been in a turmoil all his life. For all that, he destroyed many others and they didn't deserve that.'

'What you should think about now is developing your gifts properly so that you can really help others when things go wrong. It's a long hard road to take, though, and everyday problems and heartaches still have to be lived through and dealt with in your life. With the strength and knowledge the spirit world can give you, it will all be easier to get things in the right perspective. There's a saying, "God tests most those he loves the most" and my wife and I feel that He does. On the other hand, as our guides tell us, how can we help others in need if we have not trodden their path before?'

'You make life sound like an assault course,' Neil said. 'Must admit, some people do seem to have a lot more to cope with than others and this has always seemed unfair to me.'

'There are tests in our life, storms to pass through, and even if we don't know it, there's always help at hand from the spirit world. You hear some people say, "I prayed, and the answer came." Well, this is the spirit world helping us to cope, they show us the way through life's problems, but we still have a free will of our own to use, we don't have to listen, we are not puppets on a string for them to manipulate. Sometimes we don't like the way they help us because it is not what we think we should have, or what we want. Nevertheless, the results are the right ones for us, but we don't always realise that until long after. I'm hogging the conversation, so I think I'd better shut up and let you all talk amongst yourselves, but Mark and Laura, we would like you to keep in touch. We can help direct you to the right people to help develop your psychic gifts.'

Mrs Bant was sitting in an armchair, her feet on a stool. She looked exhausted, with her large blue eyes staring out of a white face.

Mark asked, 'Do you always get so exhausted, Mrs Bant? This work seems to take much out of you.'

'Yes, Mark, when it is a difficult case. They are not all traumatic like this one, most are much easier and can be completed in one sitting. We will have a break now until I am fully recovered. You need to be mentally and physically strong for this work, so we have to care for my earthly body and mind so that our work can continue. The spirit world will soon make me strong again, don't worry about me.'

The conversation passed to and fro between the others.

'I can't wait to get in there and start cleaning up. There can't be much left whole if the noises we've heard are anything to go by.' Laura felt full of energy, and was already planning what she would do.

Jack groaned. 'I'll have to keep a tight rein on you. I think you'll have the place turned inside out in no time. I'm amazed about my brother pushing me out of the way of that shell. It was the nearest I came to being dead. It was heartbreaking later on though, when we went into the concentration camps. You could hardly tell the dead from the live ones. I shan't ever forget what I saw.'

'I agree with you there,' John Oliver chipped in. 'I was only twenty years old and it's all as clear today as it was then. But fancy our little girl being around us, Fay. We go every week to her grave and I think I still will, even if she's not there, as she says. To me, it's a way of showing my love for her.'

Fay had been weeping tears of joy, remembering the message from her daughter.

'Yes, love, we'll still go,' she said. 'Mrs Bant, will she know us when we die? Won't we be too old for her to recognise us?'

'No, my dear, she'll know you because she is around you so often, and always will be, don't worry about that. Where there is love, the bond is never broken.' Mrs Bant smiled at Fay.

Neil said with a laugh, 'Don't know what the chief will think when he hears the tapes. Hope the film will be clear. We'd better watch it, Ted, he'll think we've all gone nutty, no offence to you all, of course. I've never heard anything like it. Suppose we'd better make tracks, Jerry, don't you? Early start tomorrow, and we've got reports to write before we can see the superintendent. Facts, that's what the police deal in, just facts. Come on, lad.'

Neil and Sergeant Howe were in the chief superintendent's office. The tape recorder was ready, and a screen had been set up ready for the film.

'Well, if we're ready, let's get started.' The chief sat back in his chair. He had the written reports in front of him. He was anxious to see the film that his chief inspector had been so excited about. If he had not known Neil and Sergeant Howe so well, he would have thought he was dealing with a couple of cranks. To show any form of emotion was certainly not in Howe's character.

The film was showing on the small screen, and as it progressed, the chief superintendent became more and more bemused. What he was seeing was more like a late night ghost story put on to give people nightmares. There was no sound, just the film. When it was over, he said, 'Let's see if we can get the tape to correspond with the film.'

After many stops and starts, the police operator managed this, so now he had sound as well as film.

'Damn me,' he said when it had finished. 'I'd never have believed it.'

The film that he had watched showed all that Mark had seen: the Red Indians, the African warriors, and the bows and arrows fired from them, and the spears. It was all faint but distinguishable. All the emotion on the faces of those facing the camera was clear. Even the white-robed figure leaving the body of Mrs Bant.

Neil and Sergeant Howe had seen nothing at the sitting but had heard it all. In any case, their reports concerned only the events that they had been aware of, and the sounds recorded on the tape.

'Well, according to that, we have another dead man, but no idea which river he had been pushed into. Could be anywhere. Anyway, it's years ago, and not worth chasing up, I suppose. Whoever the man belonged to would have surely reported him missing, but there are so many rivers in the British Isles it would take forever to get to the bottom of that.'

'You're right there, sir,' said Neil. 'That's why I haven't chased it up, too long ago. I found out, or rather Jerry did, how Carpenter got into his house and killed himself. Seems the place was let to a couple getting married. He broke a window and got in that way. They came back from their honeymoon to find a dead body. Couldn't and wouldn't stay there after that. Great to-do about it though, but they told the agent to take them to court. He didn't, of course. Still, they lost three months' rent money, poor little devils. What a homecoming and start to their marriage.'

'Don't think I'd have wanted to stay there, either,' replied his chief. 'I think we had better put all this in one file, and get it stored away. Close it all down, there's nothing more to be done. Opens your eyes, though, doesn't it? There are more things in Heaven and Earth than are dreamed of in our philosophy, that's for sure.'

'Sir,' Neil said, 'now that all this is cleared up, I'd like some time off. Want to give a hand to young Carpenter and his sister. His father's sister is being a bit difficult over him taking his young brother to live in his house in the Forest of Dean. Threatening him with his history, meaning his mad father, she'll try to stop him. He's a nice young lad and his sister is a cracker. I'd like to help them get sorted if it's all right with you, for time off, I mean.'

'Well, I reckon you're due for some leave. You'll be retiring soon, won't you? Better get your own affairs settled while you are about it. You are always on about a quiet place in the country to retire to. Perhaps you'll find one,' said his chief.

'I'll certainly try, Chief, I certainly will.' Neil smiled at the thought. He already knew where he wanted to go.

Chapter Thirty

Mark, Samantha and young Charlie were sitting in Neil's lounge. True to his word, Neil had asked his solicitor to come and talk to Mark.

The meal they had just eaten was delicious, and Neil was pleased that he had not lost his touch in cooking steaks.

'Used to enjoy cooking when my wife was alive, gave her a break and a complete change for me. Always good to have a change in the thought patterns. Helps to refresh you,' he said.

'It was lovely, Chief Inspector,' said Samantha. 'Dad Charlie used to do the same thing for Mum. He grew lots of vegetables, and loved bringing them fresh from the garden for Mum to cook. He was a lovely man.'

'I'm sure he was,' Neil replied. 'Anyway, I think it's time Mark and George got down to business. You can go into the dining room together, we won't disturb you. First though, I've a suggestion to make. You don't have to accept it, just think about it, all of you. What I had in mind was for you three to live with me here. Your aunt can't quibble about that with my being a chief inspector of police, can she? Along with that, young Mark, you can get on with your training in the psychic field. Mr and Mrs Bant were quite taken with you.'

'I don't understand all this,' broke in young Charlie. 'What does all this psychic thing mean? Don't tell me Mark is going to get all godly and lead us a dance. It's bad enough having Aunt Monica on at you all the time without Mark starting too.'

'Don't think he'll do that, son, anyway, we'll soon cut him down to size if he does, won't we?' Neil smiled at Charlie.

'Can we come here more? I think it's smashing here. You have a lovely garden, sir, and I could help you with it. Aunt Monica's only got a tiny yard. You can't grow anything there, it's too small.'

'Lad, you can come here whenever you like. Mind you, I'm not often here, but when I retire it will be different. We'll sort out a patch of the garden and start growing some vegetables of our own, how about that?'

'I'd like that. I tried growing things in pots in the yard, but Aunt Monica was always complaining about them, so I gave up.'

'Whatever he's tried to do, somehow it's been stopped,' Samantha said. 'He's had hurt animals, and tried to help them, but always there's been a shouting session, so he gave that up too.'

'Does that mean you'd like to be a vet, then, young Charles?' Neil asked.

'I would, but I don't see how I can,' said Charlie. 'It takes money to train. I'm good at school, but have to go up to the bedroom for peace and quiet to study. There's no peace where my aunt is concerned.'

'Well, we'll have to see about it, won't we? Now, though, your brother and George must get together and sort things out. While they do that, we'll watch television, or play draughts or cards or something, you just say. By heck, it's good to have young 'uns around.'

'I'd rather just talk,' Charlie said. 'You can't do that at home. Is it all right, Sam, if we do that?'

'Of course, Charlie, you talk away. I think you'll find the chief inspector has a good ear for listening.' Sam smiled at Neil. 'While you do that I'll wash up and, if I may, get things ready for another cup of tea for when Mark and George are finished, about an hour. Is that all right?'

'That should be fine. Come on, Mark, let's get started.' George went off to the dining room, followed by Mark.

★

They had been living with Neil for about a year. Charlie was happier than he could ever remember. To him, Neil was just like a doting grandfather. The vegetables they grew were enjoyed by all. Neil was teaching him to play golf, and he had got himself into the junior first cricket team at school. He had told Neil that he was going to call him granddad, which made Neil feel emotional. How Madge would have enjoyed having these young ones around, he thought.

Samantha was preparing for her wedding day. She was marrying the blushing young policeman she had first met in Neil's office. They had discussed having children, and Sam had said she would not have any of her own in case they turned out to be like her father. She would foster or adopt children, but would not take the risk of having a child who would be mentally sick. Still, if a child was conceived she would love it and hope for the best. This had been a blow for her fiancé Terry, but he understood her concern. He had seen too much in his work not to understand how she felt.

Sam had asked Mark if he minded her asking Neil to give her away. 'He's such a lovely father figure and we owe him so much,' she had said. So it was arranged for Mark to be Terry's best man. The wedding day dawned bright and sunny. Neil led Samantha up the aisle feeling he would burst with pride. Having no children of his own, this was something he never expected to do.

Mark had said before he left the house, 'You know, they are all gathered here. There's Madge, and our mum with Charlie and Aunt Laura. They are dressed up, so even if you can't see them, they really are here.' Sam was thrilled to think her mother and Daddy Charlie could see her, but she shed a tear just the same.

Aunt Monica had softened a little. It was difficult for her to accept that she was wanted just for herself, but all the inner bitterness remained. Financially she was secure, Mark had seen to that, so she really had nothing to grumble at, but she still did when the mood came over her. Mark understand and said, 'To show love you have to know what it is, and Aunt Monica doesn't, poor soul. She's a very bitter woman and always will be.'

Chapter Thirty-One

Mark sat in his office, dealing with the many sorrowful letters he received regularly. He was now a well-known medium and had travelled to various places in the world. It had taken him seven years of hard work to reach his full potential, and he was still learning. He knew who his spirit guides were, and there were many. He had learned very early in his training that he had a main guide, and the name he gave was Ayoha, an old man who had lived many hundreds of years ago: his skin was black, and his wisdom and compassion for all suffering humanity was without bounds. However, he could be stern when the occasion demanded it.

There was also a monk who had in Earth life cared for the sick of the monastery. Through his help, Mark had been able to help many people with emotional and physical illnesses. 'All spiritual healing is channelled through you like an energy force,' he had told Mark.

Mark had many other guides, including children, who called him Daddy. Some had been abused and murdered, some had been loved dearly, but they all came in their child form, even though some had passed to the spirit world many years before.

Mark learned about karma, his past lives, and learned how to regress people back through their own previous lives. He learned that one's karma was lived throughout the many lives one lives on Earth. Reincarnation was chosen by some because they wished to serve their fellow human beings, or because they had a purpose to complete which they had not fulfilled in their previous lives. It amazed him to learn how many previous lives he had lived, even back to prehistoric times, and that in many he had passed to spirit at a young age. He had been born into his present traumatic karma at his own choice so that he would be able to help others who had suffered.

The colours he could see around everyone and every living thing which he learned was called the aura, and as a child thought everyone could see, he now understood. When people first came to him sick in mind or body, their aura would be dull, pale, and in some cases quite narrow, even broken for those who were very sick. It gave him a lift to see the colours brightening and widening until they became vibrant. Not everyone could be helped, of course, and he had learned to accept this. Some people needed only a few visits but others needed help for quite a long while.

He also had pupils of his own now, and tried hard to train them with compassion, for some had only understood their psychic abilities because of some traumatic incident in their lives.

One of the greatest joys in his life was going into a fairly new building called Charles Lambert House. This was a haven for battered wives and abused children. He understood the mental state of the children only too well, because of his own memories. Some women were withdrawn, and some were loud in their complaints, which made their children more disturbed.

On rare occasions, men came with their children because they knew they had to get them to a place where they would be secure. Mark dealt with them all as best he could, and always there were professional counsellors ready to come in. Mostly, the home was used by the occupants until they could be accommodated in a new home of their own, but some returned to their husbands. Many were full of fear in case their husbands found them, but the other women all banded together to help them over this.

Mark's greatest helper had been Neil, who came to live with him. His down-to-earth manner and kindly nature helped to soothe many fearful women and children. Neil, however, was getting on in years and needed a quiet retirement.

When Nanny Dowers had died, Mark had purchased her cottage and extended it, bringing the two homes together. He and Neil lived in a flat on the ground floor, overlooking the back garden.

Mark missed Nanny Dowers, she had been part of his life for so long it felt strange not having her around. He often saw her in spirit form, and this did a great deal to ease his sense of loss.

Chapter Thirty-Two

Mark was now forty years old. Charles Lambert House ran on voluntary contributions, plus part of his earnings. Neil was no longer able to help, and regular staff had had to be appointed. Mark chose the staff carefully, studying every part of their character. There were only two, and they came from the village. The residents had to care for themselves and their children, and help each other when required. It had to be this way because Mark wanted Charles Lambert House to continue as a haven of rescue long after he passed to the spirit world.

Sam and Terry were settled, and had had a child after all. His half-brother, Charlie, had also married and had three children. He had trained to be a veterinary surgeon, and was practising in Gloucester.

Mark had not married, his life being completely taken up with his work, and he had never met a girl ready to accept that. I suppose one day I'll meet the right person, he thought, and Ayoha had said, 'Yes, my son, there is a woman for you, and she will come into your life through your work.'

One day, there came into Charles Lambert House a dark-haired woman with three children. All had the marks of sustained violence on them. When he went to greet them, the children backed away in fear, and the mother, as ill as she was, stirred herself ready to defend them.

'Oh, my God,' Mark said to her. 'You look just like my mother did when we first came here with Charlie Lambert. Don't be afraid of me please, I promise I won't hurt you, I want to help you. I know how you feel because I went through the same thing many years ago when I was a little boy. Come, let me show you to your room where you can rest and be treated for your injuries.' He looked at the children clinging to their mother. 'Truly, I won't hurt you ever, no one will, ever again, little ones. After a while here, you will all feel better than you do now.'

The young woman opened her mouth to speak but there was no sound. Her knees buckled under and down she went, oblivious to everything. The children were crying loudly in their fear, and the eldest, a little girl, threw herself on her mother, crying, 'Get up, Mummy, please get up,' her little body racked with sobs.

Mark called for help as he lifted the young woman into a wheelchair. He asked one of his helpers, Doris, to look after the children until he had put the woman into bed, and then to bring them in. By this time, other residents had come forward. 'Leave her to us, Mark, we'll get her settled and we'll see to the children.'

Mark led them to a room with three beds in it. 'I'll get some tea and fruit juice and will bring it when you have settled them in.'

'Right, Mark. Poor soul, God, she's taken a beating,' one young woman said. 'We were all like this once, weren't we? What a life, but I can tell you this: no man will ever do that to me again, or to my kids. Come on then, let's go and get her sorted.'

Mark looked down on the woman now lying in a bed. He felt his heart would break, for as he looked at her, he saw not her face, but the face of his mother as it had been when they first entered this house. He understood only too well the fear the children felt.

Charlie, he thought, your home is surely a haven for these poor souls. And the answer came back, 'Look after her, Mark, she will be yours to care for one day and the children will call you Daddy Mark, just like you called me Daddy Charlie. Just be patient.'

'Yes, Charlie, you are right, I feel it. I did not think one could fall in love at first sight, especially with one so battered about the face. Another man just like my father, I would think.'

Charlie replied, 'Worse, Mark. Her husband is a murderer many times over.'

Dear God, thought Mark. What a world we live in.

'Yes, my son, and you have to bring some love and peace into it with your work.' And this time the voice was that of Ayoha.

Chapter Thirty-Three

Helen and her children – Julie aged ten years, David eight, and Vicky seven – looked the picture of health. They had been in the home for three years now. The haunted look had gone from their faces but the memories would never leave them.

As the bruising and swelling had gradually left Helen's face and body, her natural beauty showed. Her hair, however, was streaked with grey. She was thirty-two years old, but felt she had lived a dozen lives in one. The divorce from her husband had not been a problem and her husband was now confined in an institution for the criminally insane, from which he would never be free. At least I hope he'll never be free to murder again, Helen thought. The children he had killed were numerous and their injuries horrific. Thank God I got my children away in time.

As they got to know Mark better, Helen and her children felt more and more safe and at peace. They were now married and she felt a contentment she had never known before and had never believed possible. Mark had explained about his psychic work and why he felt that nothing must interfere with it.

'It's not a job, dear, it's more a way of life,' he had told her. 'I feel I have been given so much since Charlie came into our lives, and then Neil, that it can only be right to give to others in return.' Mark had gone on to tell her about his life, and when he came to explain how his mother had been when he first met Charlie, she could see how it affected him. The horror of seeing the remains of Charlie, whom he'd loved and respected so much, he would never forget. 'But then, you see, it's easier for me than for most other people because I see and hear him, so it's a bit like talking to him on the telephone.'

To Helen, he was someone very special and she made sure that he was never disturbed in his work. Neil lived with them and took on a grandfather role. Although his physical capabilities were not as good, his mind was still as sharp as a razor and he spent much time with the children, helping with their lessons and teaching them all he had learned about the countryside.

'I think Vicky will be a vet when she grows up,' Neil had told Helen. Vicky was fond of bringing injured birds and sometimes rabbits to him, and together they treated them if it was possible, or took them to the local vet if that was necessary. Certainly, Vicky seemed to have an affinity with animals that the others didn't have. They now had a cat and a dog which they'd fetched from a nearby animal shelter, and they were more Vicky's than anyone's.

As the women and their children, and sometimes a man and his children, came to the home, Helen found herself a role as receptionist and comforter. She could empathise very well with these poor distressed souls and tried hard to bring some peace to them.

'I sometimes think that family violence is on the increase,' she'd said to Mark one day.

'No,' he had replied. 'It's just that it's come out into the open more. It all used to be swept under the carpet, but it is good that violence in the home is now being dealt with openly. It is hoped that the same cycle of events will be prevented. If all you have ever known in the home is violence and abuse, you have to be shown that it need not be.'

Mark had commissioned a portrait of Daddy Charlie to be painted from a photograph. This hung in the front hall of the home, and the face seemed to smile benignly down from the frame.

'That is where he should be,' said Mark to Helen. 'Looking down with love upon all who come here in need. It is a fitting epitaph for Daddy Charlie.'